KLITZMAN'S PAWN: BOOK ONE

A Harry Wiggins Novel

By

PAUL BLADES

Cover Art by Agnes Knox
agnesknox@simonas.se
agnes.knox@gmail.com

Dark Visions Publications
darkvisionspub@gmail.com

Other books by Paul Blades:

Klitzman's Isle
Klitzman's Empire
Klitzman's Paradise
The Taking of Cheryl Part One
The Taking of Cheryl Part Two: Slaver's Bait
Comfort Girl No. 4
Sacrifice to the Emerald God
The Blue Cantina: Anna's Surrender

The Maddy Saga:

Vol. I	Maddy Become a Ponygirl
Vol. II	The Training of a Ponygirl
Vol. III	Ponygirl Champion
Vol. IV	Ponygirl Summer
Vol. V.	Ponygirl Love
Vol. VI	Ponygirl Season
Vol. VII	Ponygirl Gambit
Vol. VIII	Ponygirl Pleasures
Vol. IX	Ponygirl Peril
Vol. X	Ponygirl's Choice

CHAPTER ONE

It's not something that you see every day. I mean you, not me. Unless you live with two beautiful, compliant, subservient young women who'll do anything you say anytime you want. In fact, most times, here on Klitzman's Isle, I get to see it several times a day, not that I ever get tired of it.

The spotlight was shining directly on the two young, naked, writhing, impassioned women on the small stage in the middle of the otherwise dimly lit room. They had been at it for about ten minutes. The one on top, I think her name was Donna or Dolores or something like that, I can't really remember, was a long legged brunette. She had long, chestnut colored hair that ran down to her waist as straight as a waterfall. Her legs were spread wide and she had her face buried in the fevered quim of the smaller, blond haired girl who was, in turn, frantically slurping at the exposed, dripping, hairless slit of the energized woman above her. The blond girl's arms were circled tightly around the backs of the brunette's thighs holding her pussy poised firmly in place for her ministrations. Her hair was short cropped and formed little, golden ringlets on her head. I could see her long tongue darting energetically along the length of the brunette's slit and then down to her hardened pleasure bud. Each time she got there she gave the little nubbin a long, languorous suck that made the brown haired girl squirm and moan.

The blond, a thin, dainty breasted girl named Vicki, who I knew well, was herself emitting little, staccato moans and I could see her raised knees and her bright red, high heeled shoes as they stomped and dragged on the padded surface of the stage in apparent frustration. The brunette's thin, straight hair was splayed across her sweat covered back, and from my vantage point I could see her twitching rear cheeks and the inviting, pale brown star of her nether entrance. On her right buttock, high up, just below her hip, she wore a bright red, cursive '*k*' burned into her flesh.

The girls were engaged in a sort of contest. Not that it was their idea, of course. Little that happened to slave girls on Klitzman's Isle was their idea. From what I could tell, it was the idea of Mr. Cho Jung Min, President and chief operating executive of the Dungbu International Trading Co., Ltd. He and the other members of the Board of Directors were celebrating an unusually profitable quarter for the South Korean conglomerate. There were six of them, not counting the obsequious, little, squinty eyed guy who had spent the evening relaying the curt, excited demands of the other men in English to the women who were serving them.

The party had been going on since about 8 o'clock in one of the party rooms of the guest quarters, me, dressed in my reddish brown robe denoting my role as a supervisor, them in their pale blue robes marking their status as guests. There had been a lavish banquet served by the six beautiful and naked slave girls assigned to them for the night. Scotch whiskey had flowed like water and the grizzled, elderly men had begun the evening as sedate but excited gentlemen of wealth and power but had degenerated into wild and crazy frat boys after about an hour and a continuous series of toasts to the chairman, Mr. Cho.

Rukimo, the mountainous black man who ran the day to day operations of the island, had assigned me to the group to make sure that they enjoyed themselves but did not get out of hand. Abuse of the serving wenches was expected, but the last time these boys were here they had exceeded even the generous bounds of propriety that governed behavior at this perverse resort. The expense of the woefully damaged slave girls had been added to their tab of course, but those kinds of things were frowned upon as being bad for the morale of the girls who, after all, were only human, and could not be expected to be at their best and brightest if they had to anticipate ending their work shifts being hauled out on a stretcher.

The game was simple, really. The girls were instructed to gemauch either other on the stage. The winner was the one who could hold off her orgasm the longest. To her was awarded the privilege of taking her turn at the chairman's dick, sucking at his wizened, Viagra encouraged pole until he came. The loser would be unceremoniously hauled up by her ankles and tied off to a bar dangling from the ceiling, feet wide apart, and treated to a fierce and energetic lashing by members of the Board.

The loser of the last round, a buxom redhead with firm, mare-like thighs, was still dangling upside down at the side of the stage, her pale skin striped with the lattice-like results of her ordeal, her reddish orange tresses trailing underneath her almost to the floor. One of the men was standing up against her, taking advantage of her widespread thighs and sucking eagerly at her bruised, plump, hairless mons while plunging his thick tool into her mouth. He had hold of her orange tinted hair behind her head and was pumping her mouth back and forth eagerly on his cock. Her hands had been locked behind her before she was beaten and she was defenseless to regulate the man's tempo or the depths of his penetration of her mouth and throat. Her garbled protestations as she struggled for breath, emitted as a kind of "Ga! each time the hard wand of flesh penetrated her esophagus, mingled with the moans and grunts of the struggling girls on the platform in a kind of melodic counterpoint.

I was seated in one of the padded swivel chairs that surrounded the two foot high rounded stage. My rust colored robe was drawn open and I was enjoying the patient and skilled lips of a diminutive, brown haired, ponytailed girl. I had instructed her not to let me come, but rather, to keep me on the edge of completion while I took in the spectacle. My hand was resting softly on her head as she gave me languorous strokes of my cock with her well practiced lips while her large, round, doe like eyes peered up at me, carefully measuring my excitement. It was getting harder and harder not to succumb to the warm, wet delectations of her mouth. I was woozy from all of the booze, more than I would normally take in, and my resolve to reserve my sexual energies for later was swiftly dissipating.

If it was difficult for me to reign in my urge to orgasm, it was torture for the girls on the stage. Slave girls on Klitzman's Isle were trained to a pinnacle of sexual responsiveness. Several weeks in Rukimo's underground training cells was usually sufficient to turn the most reticent and demure young ladies into fevered and fervent sluts. Rukimo's uniformly huge, black African guards were expert at drawing out sexual passion from the unfortunate young women who found their way there and nobody graduated until she could will herself into lustful response at the drop of a hat or, if not, at the unfurling of a long, vicious bull whip.

And so Vicki and Donna or Denise, or whatever her name was, were fighting off what had become their basic nature as they tried to resist the expert application of their opponent's tongue and lips. It was hard to tell who was winning. I could see the brunette's thighs struggling in the blond girl's grip as she instinctively tried to close them to deny her assailant access to her center of pleasure. Vicki's squeals and moans were getting louder and more desperate. I wondered idly whether being on top or on bottom was more advantageous in delaying the effects of the well trained and energetic mouths that was scouring each other's loins. The redhead who was having her mouth used like a cunt had been on bottom, but the blond girl who had lost the first round and who was still dangling from her ankles in the corner of the room recovering from the effects of the four foot long leather quirts that the members of the Board of Directors had wielded with such gusto as they administered the penalty for her loss of self control, had been on top.

The contest between Vicki and the long haired brunette was coming to a crisis. I could see that Vicki's grip on the brunette's legs had become tighter as if she was holding on to them for dear life. Her slender fingers, tipped by long, bright red, painted nails were making little dimples in the soft flesh of the brunette's pale, soft thighs. The brunette's moans had become deep and prolonged and I could see her head bobbing frantically up and down. The cheeks of her ass had accelerated their twitches in her excitement and her rear entrance was clenched tight. The Koreans had apparently sensed that the race was about over and were screaming and yelling for their favorites.

All of a sudden, Vicki gave out a piteous, frustrated scream. Her head rolled back and her ruby colored lips parted in a wide 'O'. Her face was strained and flushed bright red. Her knees, which had been spread wide, closed tightly against the head that was tormenting her and her legs began to flail. "Oh! Oh! Oh! Ohhhhhhhh!" she yelled as her orgasm overtook her. "Oh God! Oh! Oh! Oh!" she yelled in pleasure and frustration. Three of the Koreans erupted into raucous cheers while the other three gave out moans and shouts of disappointment.

Vicki was shaking and shuddering underneath the brunette, but the other girl was showing her no mercy. She continued her attentions to the throbbing pussy beneath her. Vicki had abandoned her efforts at the luscious quim of her adversary and her face was contorted with the evidence of her launch into sexual oblivion.

Chairman Cho, who has sitting to my right with a black haired slave girl bent over his knees, his hand worrying the distended gap between her outstretched thighs, barked a staccato, series of harsh sounding words to the other men. They had discarded their pale blue robes and were dancing and jumping around the stage, scotch filled glasses in hands, like school boys waiting for ice cream. Joo-Chan, the reserved and taciturn factotum, still dressed primly in his knee length, pale blue robe, yelled out his master's command to the two women to break apart.

The brunette, who, like most successful slave girls on the island, had remained keyed to the voice of male authority even while engaged in the fevered contest with the blond girl, immediately lifted her torso up from the girl's still writhing body and rolled off of her. Her face was smeared with the proof of Vicki's orgasm and was etched with the evidence of her own arousal, her lips engorged and parted, her eyes wide and moist. Her chest above her bounteous breasts was reddened and her nipples stood up like soldiers at attention. Her breath was heavy and labored and as she took a seated position on the stage next to her unfortunate sister, her legs spread wide and her knees bent, I could sense her roused lust and bittersweet disappointment that she had not been allowed its fruition. Her hands stroked her long, well toned thighs in frustration as if begging for permission to address her flowered, lust laden crevasse. But it was not to be, not yet anyway, as Joo-Chan ordered her to pay obeisance to the Chairman's prick.

Two of the Koreans, their delight in having selected the winner in the contest obvious, and eager to reap their reward of the right to administer a beating to the loser, had grabbed the blond girl's ankles and were lifting her bodily up into the air. The Korean men were all well over sixty, but they had retained the well muscled bodies of their youths and were able to raise Vicki's body without noticeable effort. They were laughing and smiling as they affixed the leather bracelets around the girl's ankles to the bar that had been dangling over the stage like the sword of Damocles, spreading the unfortunate girl's legs widely. A third man pulled on the chain that held the bar aloft and raised it higher until the girl's head was lifted off of the soft surface of the stage and she was suspended in air.

Vicki's long, thin body was shiny with the sweat of her recent exertions. Her arms dangled below her and her hands were desperately seeking purchase on the smooth stage surface to deny the efforts of her captors. Once they had her in the air, however, they quickly grabbed her arms and confined her wrists behind her by clasping her two leather bracelets together.

The girls on Klitzman's Isle were no strangers to the whip. But it was one thing to be fastened across a stanchion ready to receive the steady, well timed strokes of a deserved beating. It was another to be the victim of a lash wielded by a patron in the throws of passion. Vicki's face recorded her dismay and fear as she swung helplessly from the elevated bar. Her lips were tightly pressed together and tears had already begun to well up in her eyes. She looked at me beseechingly.

Like I said, I knew Vicki well. She had served as a waitress for a time in the jazz lounge that I ran on the resort for the benefit of the guests. I had developed, quite unintentionally, a reputation among the slave girls for a muted sympathy for their plight. I rarely beat any of them for pleasure beyond the few strokes that were sufficient to get my fires going. And I tried to treat them with a deference for their unhappy, involuntary fates. Vicki loved to fuck and, after the bar had closed for the night, I had a few times brought her back to my cottage for an evening's entertainment. The girl had saucy features and a lithe frame. Although not of sufficient beauty to serve as one of the lounge girls, girls who, dressed in fashionable but revealing attire and gave pretense to my establishment as a ordinary watering hole, waiting to be picked up by the 'handsome' strangers who happened in, she was good natured and her sexual skills had received favorable mention more than once. She had lost her job in one of the many shuffles of slave girl duties that occurred on the island. No girl should think that any of her assignments were permanent and it was only fair that she be thrown back into the pool, so to speak, after a few weeks as a plaything at my bar.

I knew that Vicki's forlorn gaze was not an appeal for my intervention. She knew better than that. But it was a plea for sympathy and, perhaps, a nostalgic entreaty for the safer, more sedate atmosphere of my jazz lounge. As I fought off the mesmerizing effects of the soft, hot tongue that was circumnavigating my cock, I promised myself that I would try and give the poor girl a few days of respite from her duties in the resort proper if I could.

Having positioned the long, languorous body of the girl where they wanted her, the Koreans retrieved their quirts from the floor where they had dropped them after the last round of beatings and prepared for their assault on Vicki's tender flesh. I could see the inside of the girl's thighs quivering in dreadful anticipation of their ordeal. She was giving out a mournful moan and her upside down breasts swayed and jiggled enticingly as they were shifted about by her heaving chest.

The first blow was struck by a heavyset, muscular Korean with short cut, salt and pepper hair. He had drawn the offensive instrument back and brought it down directly on the parted and still oozing sex of the girl. Vicki gave out a great howl as her delicate pussy received the thin, stiff, leather strap. A line of bright red emerged instantly. Her body quaked and writhed and her motions made her torso swing unsteadily. The first blow was followed quickly by a second from another lust filled Korean and then a third and a fourth.

The room was filled with the anguished screams of the poor girl as her body twisted and turned in a fruitless effort to avoid her torment. Long red lines were appearing all over her as the three Korean men assailed her relentlessly. Chairman Cho was sitting blithely in his chair, a cruel smile spread over his face as he, in turn, received the oral attentions of the brunette. Joo-Chan was crouched behind her, giving her already steaming cunt the attentions of his hand as he drove her lusts higher and higher. I could hear her moans and energetic slurps at Cho's dick as Vicki received a rain of excruciating blows from the other men's whips. The poor girl's voice was getting hoarse as she begged and pleaded for the men to stop. Pleas for mercy from slave girls were usually strictly verboten as they were expected to accept meekly what their masters doled out, but I decided not to report the poor, golden haired girl, as her circumstances were extreme, even as judged by normal island standards.

My own lusts were rising higher and higher. I had wanted to save all of my sexual energies for my two favorite slave girls, Carol and Mary, who were awaiting my pleasure in my cottage. I had been somewhat inattentive to their needs lately and I had promised an evening of delight to them when I had left my cottage that morning and dropped them off, as usual, at the Slave Center. They usually spent their days there exercising, helping the new girls become acclimatized to their fates and honing their own sexual skills. I knew that from time to time they would be required to service the big African guards who served there or the pleasures of one of the slave supervisors who happened down to the underground facility. But it was better than having them chained up in my cottage all day.

The Slave Center was to be distinguished from Rukimo's domain. It was where the slave girls lived and trained after they had been broken in at Rukimo's. There were on the island between a hundred and a hundred and fifty beautiful slave girls at any given time and they, naturally, needed some place to sleep, exercise and make themselves pretty for their service above ground. Newly trained girls went there for indoctrination and were sometimes sold to off island buyers from there directly. It was run by the cruel and beautiful Madam Dupre, who took great pleasure in administering the whip to her charges and satisfying her own never ending Sapphic desires.

All thoughts of my promises to Mary and Carol were going swiftly by the boards. My juices were rising and the sight of Vicky's torment, even though I rued her obligation to endure it, was sending waves of lust through my body. The hand that I had left resting comfortably on the pretty head of the girl at my cock took a grip on her finely combed, convenient ponytail and I began to urge her to completion of her efforts. I could feel the tell tale sensations of my lust coming over boil and I closed my eyes to better savor the last few moments of almost tortuous bliss before my explosion. Vicki's desperate, woeful pleas for surcease and the distinctive sound of leather hitting flesh flooded my ears as my cock began to throb and spurt in ecstasy. My mind clouded over as the convulsions of my cock sent wave after wave of pleasure to my brain. I could feel my fluids flowing down my rigid pole at each pulse. I gave out a loud, deep groan as the sensations overwhelmed me.

As my ejaculations slowed, my awareness of the others in the room began to return. One of the Koreans had pulled the black haired girl from Mr. Cho's lap and was fucking her energetically on the stage. Another had seized the only other 'free' girl in the room, a dark skinned Latina rather new to her collar, and was doing her doggy style on the floor. The third Korean from the losing team had lowered the blond hair girl who had gone first onto the floor and was deeply engaged in her nether hole, pounding his hips at her fiercely and making the girl cry out with pain.

The three winners had finally done with Vicki. Her body was crisscrossed with the evidence of her travail and she was crying and moaning as her body swung gently to and fro. The men lowered the bar from which she hung and released her. She fell onto the stage with a dull thud, unable to break her fall due to her confined wrists behind her back. She was quickly pulled to her knees and one of the Koreans, the one who had commenced her vicious beating, grabbed her short, curly golden blond hair, bent her over so that her marred, tortured breasts were crushed by her wounded thighs and forced himself between her lips. Another mounted her from behind and the two men began to pump their cocks into her in a frenzy.

The third Korean who had been whipping Vicki politely bowed to me and made a curt but pleasantly toned inquiry in Korean. Joo-Chin quickly translated the man's request. It seems that he saw that I was finished with the ponytailed girl's mouth and was seeking my indulgence at letting him have her next 'dance'. I nodded to him deferentially and he grabbed the two foot long skein of soft, thin hair behind her head and dragged her over to the stage. He laid her back down on it, raised her thighs and plunged himself immediately into her cleft. Luckily for her that she had kept it moist and ready and the grey haired, powerful man had no trouble in sinking himself within her to the hilt.

I could see that the Koreans were well occupied and I took the opportunity to rise from my chair and return to the table where we had feted. My glass was still half full of diluted scotch and soda, a sin that I would not ordinarily have committed, but the Koreans had insisted on a commercial blend rather than one of the single malt scotches that I preferred. I took a long sip, enjoying the sensation of the alcohol melding with my relaxed, satisfied physical state.

The room was a cacophony of moans and grunts as the Korean men plied their passions among the obediently lustful slave girls. I looked over at Joo-Chin and wondered what it was going to take to get the Chairman's major domo to succumb to the wave of degenerate passion that was flowing through the room. He was looking down calmly at the shuddering, moaning brunette who was servicing his master and lord, rubbing and probing her enflamed loins dispassionately. Besides me, he was the only one who was still clothed. He looked up at me impassively for an instant and I sensed his steely nerves and ambition. He might be the servant of the Chairman for now, but I sensed a cold, calculating confidence in his eyes, unashamed at his subservient role, for now at least. Soon, I felt, when he had figured out how to unseat Mr. Cho, the other men in the room would be bowing and scraping to him.

Suddenly Mr. Cho gave a loud, shrill grunt signaling his successful conclusion of his orgasm. The brunette allowed herself release and she issued muffled cries and moans as she received the Chairman's creamy spunk in her mouth. The other men were engaged in concluding their business too and one by one they gave out their exclamations of passion and then slumped over the bodies of their victims. The women were resolving their lusts as well and I could hear their shrill, feminine voices crying out in satisfaction.

Cho rudely pushed aside the brunette who had been servicing him and barked out a command. The members of the Board of Directors of the Dungbu International Trading Co., Ltd. obediently struggled to their feet. It was the signal that the party was over. One by one the men retrieved their knee length, pale blue robes and donned them. There was much muted laughter and the slapping of backs as they prepared to leave. Not that their night was over. Back in the guests' dormitory there would be compliant and expectant slave girls waiting for them, an accommodation of the house. If the men hadn't yet satisfied their lusts completely, or worn out the effects of their doses of Viagra, there was more entertainment ahead.

Mr. Cho gave me a slight, respectful bow in thanks for my attendance at their celebration, which I returned dutifully, careful to bow my head just a little bit lower then his. The other executives made their polite acknowledgements and the men all shuffled out of the party room.

Tired and worn out slave girls lay about the room like discarded party favors. It was my job to get them all back on their feet and secure them for their happy journey back to the Slave Center. Their travails were over for the evening and they could look forwards for the relative safety of their dorm. I eased the red headed slave to the floor. She had been left hanging from her ankles during the finale of lust that had topped off the evening. The other girls assembled dutifully in a little line and I began to fix their wrists behind their backs and adorn them with their travel gags.

No slave girl was permitted to walk freely around the resort and they were required to be bound and gagged while doing so. The girls would shuffle their way on their pretty high heeled feet back to the Slave Center in a coffle with their destination marked clearly on a tag around the lead girl's neck. They would be strictly timed and one of the delights of the resort was watching a line of naked and harried females, all dressed in nothing but their bright red high heeled shoes, their stiff leather collars and their slave bracelets around their wrists and ankles, clip clopping their way hurriedly to their destination, their swaying, naked breasts recording each well timed step.

I had administered all of the girls' gags and had bound all of their arms behind them when I noticed that I was not the only man in the room. Joo-Chin was sitting in the dim light at the table where we had had our feast and was downing a glass of scotch. Apparently his duties for the night were at an end as well. He slowly rose to his feet and approached me.

"I thank you for a very entertaining evening on behalf of Mr. Cho and the members of the Board," he said politely. His voice was soft and accommodating, he having resumed his disguise as a mere servant of his master. I had just connected the hands of the brunette, Darla or Donna, whatever her name was, to the collar of the red headed girl and was about to fix the diminutive ponytailed girl behind her. She, like the other girls had received her gag willingly, almost thankfully. She had a pleasant, almost child like face and her limpid, large brown eyes peered back at me happily, communicating her gratitude that she had escaped her night of abuse relatively unscathed.

"Please, Mr. Wiggins, if I may interrupt you. I would like to take that one back to my room. It is permitted I understand."

I stepped back from the small, frail girl. "Of course," I answered. The girl gave out a little whine, not loud enough for the guest to hear, but loud enough for my detection. I had already attached the 18" long chain to her collar and I gave it a little tug to pull the girl from the line. Joo-Chin took it from me and then leaned over and picked up one of the quirts that the other men had left behind on the floor.

I realized that the girl was in for a whole evening of shit. I felt sorry for her, having survived the cunnalingual contest only to end up with the booby prize of a night of terror and pain with the cold, calculating Joo-Chin. I could see her tremble and the beginning of tears in her eyes. I tried to dissuade him.

"You are aware, of course that there is a slave girl awaiting you in your room who will be more than happy to let you act out your every desire with her?" I asked.

"Oh, yes, oh yes," Joo-Chin answered. His eyes were wandering over the dainty flesh of the girl and he had seized of her pert, delicate breasts with his free hand. "It's just that I have been admiring this one all night, Mr. Wiggins. Her body seems to have been just made for the whip. I watched her while she serviced you and my mind kept imagining her exquisite cries and screams. Mr. Cho has promised me that I may acquire one of your well trained sluts and bring her back with us to Korea. I think that I have found the one I want." He gave the girl's breast a harsh pinch and her pretty, doleful, frightened eyes winced in pain.

I had a moment's thought to continue to try and dissuade him from selecting the girl, but then I thought better of it. Clearly one of the girls was going back to Korea with this cold hearted, cruel man. If it was not this girl it would be another. By saving her I would be condemning someone else. Few of the beautiful young women who had been kidnapped from their homelands and brought to this isle of pain off the African coast deserved their fate. I was certain that this pretty, doll-like creature did not either. But to seem too concerned with her fate would possibly reflect on my bona fides as a ruthless, callous criminal. I had worked hard to fit into the milieu of Klitzman's Island and had steeled myself to its cruelty. I had refused to give up my cover for females who I had known better and longer than the little ponytailed girl and would not do so for her now.

"As you please," I answered the thin, hard eyed Korean.

I watched as Joo-Chin marched from the party room, the unfortunate little ponytailed girl struggling to keep up as he led her by the chain affixed to her collar. She had given me one last desperate look before she was led away and I felt a swell of pity for her. But it only lasted a moment. My last sight of her was her bound, writhing little hands behind her and her tight, well rounded ass, the bright red '*k*' burned into it proclaiming her as Klitzman's property to do with and dispose of as he wished. I guess Joo-Chin found her to his liking since I never did see her again.

CHAPTER TWO

I turned to the other females who were standing there waiting obediently for me to finish. I thought I could detect a look of relief in their eyes as well as a look of appreciation for my unfruitful efforts on behalf of their sister slave. I gave myself a little kick as I realized that I had done it again. The opportunity for the slave girls to communicate with each other was slim and heavily regulated. They had no real need to exchange information beyond what was strictly necessary to fulfill their servile functions. I had come to realize that a kind of underground communication system was in effect between them and news of the occasional acts of kindness that I had committed in my role as a supervisor had spread. It was not the tough, cruel reputation that I craved. All I needed was to create more suspicion about myself. If Klitzman or Rukimo ever discovered that I was a viper in their bosom, an agent of an unnamed US government security agency, I would die a very slow, painful death.

I guess it's time for me to introduce myself for those of you who are not familiar with my tale. My name is Harry Wiggins. I'm 35, about 6' tall and big enough to handle myself in most kinds of tough guy situations. I'm self aware enough to know that I was never the brightest bulb in the chandelier, but I wasn't the dimmest either. I had misspent my youth and early adulthood as a sort of low level, one man crime wave. I was born and bred in Bayonne, New Jersey and had drifted out to California in my early twenties to seek new opportunities in a place where the cops didn't know me so well. I had been tripped up on a b&e of a jewelry store in Bakersfield and had, because of my New Jersey record, been sentenced to a three year bid in Vacaville State Prison. There I met a guy, who knew a guy, who was friends with a guy who could set me up with a real organization back in New Jersey. And that's how I met Tony Bianco.

Life with Tony was sweet. I did some collection work for him, learned to handle a .45 and soon graduated to his inner circle. Tony was heavy into loan sharking, prostitution, drugs and the other cottage industries of organized crime. Once in a while a competitor, a debtor too far gone to ever pay him back, or someone who Tony had grown suspicious about, had to shuffle off their mortal coil. It didn't happen too often, but I have to confess that I was the last thing that more than one guy saw before he met his maker. I earned a good buck, had regular access to Tony's stable of party girls and got to spend some time at the beach. Everything was hunky dory until one day the FBI poked their noses into our affairs.

I was caught red handed doing a fuck up named Jimmy Tiger who had welshed on Tony. It was all part of a huge racketeering investigation and me and Jimmy were being monitored on tape. If the FBI had been just a little more perspicacious about protecting their informant, Jimmy and I could have had a big laugh about it one day. The judge didn't think it was funny at all and while Tony and the other boys got off with 10's and 20's, I got life.

I had thought that my life was for all practical purposes over. Tony's promises to take care of me quickly evaporated as he was sent to a minimum in Texas and I was sent to the max in Atlanta. My future life loomed before me as being brutish, nasty and short. But after a little more than three years of hard time, I had been recruited while at the penitentiary by two guys named Bederson and Mulattieri. They told me, or rather Bederson did, he did all the talking, that they represented a "confidential", Bederson never did use the word 'secret', government agency that was investigating an international criminal organization known only by the initial '*k*'. I had never heard of it.

I hadn't had a single visitor in the three and a half years since my sentencing and was looking forwards to many, many years of drudgery and institutional haircuts. I didn't relish being a snitch and knew that if I was caught I would be dead meat. But everybody's gotta die sometime and I didn't want to spend my next thirty or forty years shitting in the same toilet in the same 8x10' cell and sleeping on the same 2 ½ inch thick, cotton pallet. So I said, "What the fuck." Bederson said that there was important national security matters involved, but I didn't give a rat's ass about that. What I cared about was that he also said that anything I did criminal-wise while on assignment for the government would be forgiven. Anything.

I worked my way into friendship with the organization's man in the pen by terminating the life force of a snitch at his request. A few weeks later, they sprung me in a smoothly worked break out and I found my way to this little island in the sun. Believe me, I had no idea what I was getting into. I soon found out that '*k*' stood for Klitzman, a 350 lb. gluttonous, cruel, sybarite, who was the mastermind of a vast coterie of underworlders whose main virtues were their penchant for murder, theft, extortion, graft, drugs and the other varying vicissitudes of modern day crime. Oh, and, I forgot to mention, the enslavement of pretty, innocent, young girls to serve a world wide demand for subservient, pliant, well trained, sexual thralls. Besides being the *crème de la crème* of female pulchritude, the girls all had one thing in common, a fiery red, cursive '*k*' burned into their buttocks demarking them as having undergone a course of demeaning and dehumanizing training at Klitzman's resort. It was a singular mark of quality. And if any of the girls shopped out to the unscrupulous powerful who could afford to maintain and secure their very own private slave girl proved recalcitrant, back slid in her duties or failed to provide instant, unreserved and passionate service to her owner, she could be shipped back here, free of charge, to spend an indeterminate time in Rukimo's underground hell relearning her skills and rediscovering her motivation for blind obedience.

The worst that I had done heretofore in my lifetime of crime was to lean on a couple of show girls who had gotten too deep into Tony because of drugs or gambling to convince them that they could repay Tony on their backs in his whorehouse up in the inlet. I was, at first, shocked at the perverse paradise that I found myself drafted into. But it didn't take long for me to get with the program. My mother didn't raise any fools.

And now I thanked God for every day that I remained alive. I got my dick wet several times a day, ate the best food money could buy. Every day was a play day. I had expected Bederson to contact me so I could report on Klitzman's operations, but the only information I had received was a toll free number to call him on if I ever got the chance. Needless to say it would have been the height of imprudence to make a telephone call from the island, assuming that I could ever get access to a telephone. All communications from the island were tightly controlled and fully monitored. But did I really want to make the call anyway?

Life at Klitzman's Isle was like a bon vivant's waking wet dream. There were first run movies, a 9 hole golf course, a gym, top shelf liquor and food and a plenitude of, if not randy, at least willing, pretty, young females at one's beck and call. Why would I ever want to leave? I mean, what else could a man want?

Bederson had threatened me with nonjudicial remedies if I crossed him, but what could he do to me that Klitzman wouldn't do if he ever found out that I was a rat? On the one hand, I had all of life's perverse pleasures at my fingertips and, on the other, I had Bederson's promise that once I had completed my 'mission' I would be free. But free to do what? Return to a life of scrounging the streets for a buck? I would probably be back in prison in a year, if not sooner. I could spend my days working at carwashes, parking lots or as a bouncer at some back street titty bar, but what kind of a life would I have on a couple of hundred bucks a week? And what if Bederson conveniently 'forgot' his promise? I would be right back where I started. And for this I should risk my precious hide and give up the lifestyle of an ancient Roman senator?

I had met some of Klitzman's meanest, cruelest enforcers and saw what they did for recreation with the girls. I was sure that my fate would be far, far worse at their hands. I had had a little tussle already with one of them already, a lean, mean, bad guy named Thorndike. He and his sidekick, Cholo, a psychotic Latino who had one of those 'just give me an excuse' looks in his eyes all the time, did a lot of Klitzman's dirty work and seemed to enjoy their jobs. And then there was Anthony, a pleasant mannered fellow whose veneer of fraternity I was sure covered up a darkened soul.

And finally, there was Rukimo. Rukimo stood about 6'7" tall, had shoulders as broad as Mt. Kilimanjaro and hands as big as frying pans. A native African with skin as black as coal, he was Klitzman's executive officer, the guy who got things done and made all of the day to day decisions. When I came to the island, I was sure that Rukimo had sussed me out and that any day I would be turned over to his minions for a long, excruciating session of "fuck up Harry." But I had apparently made my bones with him and, after a few weeks, my status at the island was upgraded from a low level supervisor to one of Klitzman's inside men. Klitzman called me one of his 'go to guys." I had been given a private cottage and been gifted my very own slave girl, Carol. She had been one of Klitzman's private playthings for a while and had been pretty battered and bruised when I got her. But I nursed her shredded, whipped body back into health and she was ever grateful to me for the kindnesses I had shown her.

I had grown fond of her too. I knew that her devotion to me was at least partly a result of her fear of whatever other fate she might meet if cast into the pool of generally available slave girls on the island. The fate of the poor, little, brown haired, ponytailed girl was a case in point. Life could change very fast for a slave girl on Klitzman's Isle and hardly ever for the better. I also knew that Carol's unqualified and repeatedly expressed commitment to my pleasure was ultimately not real, but rather a product of the psychological effects of her ordeals. A sort of Stockholm syndrome. But I took it for what it was worth and enjoyed every minute of her company.

And then there was Mary. She had been brought to me the same night that I had received Carol. As opposed to Carol, who was my property as long as Klitzman had a use for me, Mary was on loan from the resort. My status entitled me to keep a slave girl on extended duty in my cottage. Mary had helped me care for Carol while she had been recovering from her ordeals as Klitzman's whipping girl and I had grown a deep affection for her as well. She had undergone her own trauma at the hands of a guest shortly after her arrival on the island and she welcomed the chance to be free from similar depredations while she was my personal body slave.

Mary had been kidnapped at the same time as Carol and the two girls bonded immediately. Every night, when I returned to my cottage, they would be kneeling expectantly in my living room awaiting the opportunity to bring me pleasure and to receive it from me or each other. Bound and gagged as they awaited my arrival, they would not have the opportunity for any play time on their own, an activity that would have been a severe breech of the rules of the island. But I often let them cavort once my initial forces had been exhausted. Their passion for each other was clearly evident as they drove each other to lust. I told you that watching two beautiful, compliant and subservient young women engaged in a mutual sexual frenzy was something I saw every day, didn't I?

It was my 'girls', as I thought of them, that were on my mind as I made my way from the guests' pavilion back to my cottage. The slaves from the party were following behind me. As I stepped out of the building, I held the door open for them and watched them quickly stream by. They had four minutes to make their way from the guests' pavilion to the entrance to the Slave Center, something they could just make if they were quick about it. I could have given them more time but I was irked that they had all looked at me with their mooning eyes in response to my effort to relieve the ponytailed girl of her night of terror. Now they would have to hurry or they would all suffer the kiss of a riding crop for being late.

I released the leash that led to the collar of the lead girl and they took off like a shot, their breasts jerking and swaying and their fine, smooth asses recording their

quickened strides. It was about a quarter mile to the
entrance to the Slave Center, but their trek would take
them around the circumference of the resort on the special
pathways devoted to transporting coffles of slave girls. It
was longer, but they were less likely to get waylaid that way
by a guest or a supervisor looking for some poontang to top
off the night. It was a tough job running on their bright red,
high heeled shoes, but if they kept their pace to a frenzied
double time, they just might make it.

It was a relatively cool, breezy night, about two in the
morning. Days on this African Capri were hot and steamy,
but there was usually a moderate breeze coming off of the
South Atlantic. It was overcast and no stars shone overhead.
A storm was coming, one of the frequent squalls that
battered the island and the air was tense with static
electricity. I was unsettled, maybe because of the weather,
the fate of the ponytailed girl or just general ennui.
Watching the ponytailed girl disappear made me think
about the tenuousness of my hold on my beloved pets. If
anything ever happened to me, of course, they would be
thrown back into the pool of female slaves or sold off to
some sadistic bastard. Klitzman provided raw material for
some of the most scurrilous whorehouses in Africa and girls
who had passed their prime or who were too much trouble
for one reason or another were often shipped off there.

But even if I survived, my hold on the girls was insecure.
Klitzman gaveth and Klitzman could taketh away. If he
wanted Carol for some reason, he would just take her, as
might any of the other supervisors such as Thorndike,
Anthony or Cholo who were above my rank. Slave girls
were fungible in the minds of the island's lords and
somebody would just provide me with another one. And as
to Mary, I didn't even have a property claim to her. If
someone decided that she was more useful somewhere else,

she would be reassigned. I might protest and complain, but any overreaction on my part would put my bone fides in doubt.

Sooner or later it would happen, I knew that. I could only hope that it would be later rather than sooner.

The rain had just started coming down in sheets when I reached my cottage. It sat on top of a high cliff and overlooked the south side of the island with a magnificent view of the ocean for miles in three directions. On a clear day you could make out Africa off to the west. At night, you could hear the crashing of the waves on the rocks some two hundred feet or so below. It consisted of four rooms, a bedroom and a kitchen, a large, sumptuously appointed living room with all the modern electronic entertainments and a small slave alcove where the girls slept when I was not in the mood for playtime or if I had brought another slave girl home with me for my bed. It wasn't the Taj Mahal, but it was sure bigger than my cell back in Atlanta.

Carol and Mary were kneeling on the thick, red rug in the living room expectantly, just where they were supposed to be. They looked up at me happily as I came through the door. My robe was drenched and I quickly stripped it off before crouching down in front of them to give them my greeting. They were both of the same body type, slender, about 5'6" tall, with well formed, ample breasts. The guy who had kidnapped them had fooled them into thinking they were being recruited for modeling assignments overseas and had picked out a brace of 20 to 21 year old girls all of the same build and of more than satisfying pulchritude. But there the similarities stopped. Carol had large brown eyes and a round, child like face. Her chestnut colored hair descended down her back in a long braid. Her lips were thin and prim and her hips were a tad wider than Mary's. She was by nature reserved and she possessed a certain sweetness and innocence even after all that she had been through.

Mary's hair was a dark as night, smooth and black and ran down to her shoulders. She had bright, blue eyes that shown and sparkled when she was happy. Her face was longer and thinner than Carol's and her lips were succulent and full. While Carols' nipples were slight and slender, Mary's were wide and fat and surrounded by silver dollar sized, dark areolas. Her breasts were rounder and fuller than Carol's and set closer together. She had a sultry mien that was tinted with an underlying sadness. Who could blame her? I had never gone into detail with the girls about their past, but I sensed an innate, superior intelligence in Mary and assumed that she had had a bright future planned out for herself before being snatched from her life and brought here. I tried not to think about stuff like that.

The girls were happy to see me, their eyes reflecting their anticipation of our evening together. They were both wearing the standard island gag, a long, thick wad of leather ensconced in their mouths attached to a wide, leather shield that covered their lips and the lower half of their faces. Their braceleted wrists were locked behind them and a chain led from one of the bracelets on their ankles to a steel ring embedded in the floor. Their knees were spread wide apart in a submissive pose and their hairless sexes beckoned to my touch. I caressed their heads and kissed them both on the forehead. "Glad to see me girls?" I asked unnecessarily. They both nodded enthusiastically.

I ran my hand over their shoulders and leaned in and gave them both kisses on their necks, just above their thick leather slave collars. They were both adorned with a luxuriant, earthy smelling perfume and its aroma, merged with the scent of their soft, inviting flesh, was compelling.

My hands roamed over their chests and caressed their breasts softly. I reveled in the heft of their firm, resilient mounds and they both gave out soft sighs as I massaged them deftly, lingering on their hardening nipples, tweaking and pulling at them until they stood stiff and tall. The girls both arched their backs presenting their orbs for my pleasure and I could see in their eyes the recording of my efforts to draw them into lust.

"Who is going to get fucked first tonight?" I asked them playfully. They both gave out little squeals from behind their gags in an effort to persuade me to give them preeminence. I decided that I would play a little variation of Chairman Cho's game. "Okay," I said, "I'm going to stroke your pretty little quims and the first one to come gets my cock first. Now, no faking, or I just might have to give you a whipping, understand?"

The girls nodded energetically. I didn't mean to be cruel, but faking an orgasm was a big no-no on Klitzman's Isle. I had given my two pets too many bad habits already and I didn't want to spoil them too much.

I drew my hands across their firm, tight bellies and took possession of their plump, hairless mons. Their skin was soft and velvety, a product of meticulous care. I took the middle finger of each hand and dragged it tenderly along their delicate slits seeking their moisture before applying my caresses to their sensitive buds of pleasure. I did not have long to wait. Both girls had spread their thighs widely to accommodate my skillful hands. When their pussy lips began to part and their sexual fluids had begun to flow, I slid my fingers inside them gathering their secretions and then spreading it over their hardened nubs at the top.

I could see the desire of my two housemates flowing over their bodies. Mary's skin was paler than Carol's and a reddish blotch was starting to develop in the area above her delectable breasts. Carol's eyes were watering and her face was becoming flushed. Both of them unashamedly pushed their now loose and flowing pussies at my hands, rocking their hips, seeking to increase the potency of my caresses. Their heat transferred to my active fingertips and the sensation of stroking their fevered crevasses was driving my lust. It was like dipping my hands into two fecund pools of delight and my mind could not help envision the pleasure I would have later encapsulating my rigid manhood deep inside one or the other of them, or both. I leaned over and took one of Carol's teats into my mouth, sucking at it long and hard until I heard her moan with passion. I then moved my head to the left and took in one of Mary's nipples, biting at it lightly until she gave a little flinch of pain and then subsuming the tip of her breast, darkened areola and all, until the black haired girl gave a groan of delight.

The picture of my pets in the throws of passion had sparked my own and my cock was sanding at rock hard attention as I watched carefully for the tell tale signs of the commencement of sexual release in the two females. I was right handed and I thought for a moment that my more pronounced dexterity in that appendage would resound to Carol's advantage. Her brown eyes were closed and what part of her face that could be seen outside of the leather shield that covered the lower half of it seemed serenely engaged in her pleasure. Mary's starry, blue eyes were open and staring back at me starkly, her facial muscles tightened. She was giving out a low, sonorous hum as she ground her luscious slit against my hand. Carol was the more vocal of the two and her squeals of delight were emanating from her confined lips.

Suddenly, Mary gave out a cry from behind her gag and her body began to quiver and shake. Her hips began to thrust frantically back and forth as she pressed her fevered slit against my hand and stroked it up and down. I heard Carol bleat a cry of disappointment as she pressed against my hand with increased vigor. But she was too late. Mary was in the full throes of her orgasm, her fine, plump breasts shaking and swaying, her black haired head tilted back in exquisite pleasure. Her eyelids were clamped closed and the strain of her delight was evident on the muscles of her face, her creased brow. I thrust my fingers deep inside her hot crevasse to check on the authenticity of her response and I could feel her pussy's walls throb and convulse against them. She had clearly won.

Carol gave out a little cry of frustration at Mary's obvious victory. In spite of her failure to launch, I decided to continue my caresses to her loins until she had achieved satisfaction. I continued to stroke Mary's sopping crevasse gently and soothingly, prolonging the aftershocks of her climax while giving Carol the added lift she needed to achieve her completion. After a very short while, the girl's body shuddered and her thighs closed upon my arm. While Mary had seemed to exalt in her throes of passion, leaning back and letting it all hang out, Carol's torso doubled over and her moans seemed as close to ones of pain as they could be. But I knew that my brown haired pet was not in pain. I had witnessed her orgasms many times. She seemed to experience her cunt's contractions throughout her entire body. It was quite an experience to be riding her flesh when she came. Her arms would wrap around you as if she were desperately holding on to life itself and her legs would entwine themselves with your thighs in an effort to draw your entire body inside her.

And she was loud. "Mmmmmmmmm! Mmmmmmmmmmm! Mmmmmmmmm!" she cried out from behind her gag. "Mmmmmmmmm!" It was a delight to witness and my cock was literally twitching in my own excitement. I decided that I needed to bury it in a hot, succulent hole as soon as possible.

I let Carol's delight wind down for a few moments. When her body had relaxed and her thighs had loosened on my hand and arm, I withdrew it and disconnected the chains that had affixed her and Mary's ankles to the ring in the floor. I loosened Mary's wrists from behind her back and she leapt forwards to me and gave me a warm, embracing hug, her arms wound tightly around my neck.

I took her arms in my hands and gently pulled them from me. "You're the winner, Mary and I'm going to give you a round fucking," I told her to her obvious glee. "Take Carol into the bedroom and chain her feet to the foot of the bed so that she can stand there and watch."

Carol gave out a little squeak of disappointment from behind her gagged lips but rose dutifully as Mary took hold of her arm and began to drag her to the bedroom. There was no spite in either of the girls, but they enjoyed teasing each other and had a sisterly competition for my attentions. Tonight, Mary was the winner who would receive the benefit of my thick, rock hard cock in her lush canal. Tomorrow, I might decide to even it up and make Mary wait helplessly while I drove Carol to a maddening frenzy of delight.

The two naked slave girls turned the corner into my bedroom quickly. I rose more leisurely, stroking my hardened member with my hand, contemplating the pleasures which it would soon bring to me. When I entered the bedroom, Mary was crouched down by the foot of the bed busily affixing the leather bracelets around Carol's ankles to chains that led to the legs of the bed frame. Carol looked up at me forlornly, her big brown eyes supplicative of her desire to be permitted to participate in the fornication to come. I smiled at her, enjoying the idea of her beckoning eyes helplessly taking in the tableau of lust that was soon to be unfolded before her.

Mary quickly rose from her task and presented herself to me, her blue eyes filled with delightful anticipation of our upcoming romp. Her fine breasts quivered slightly as she stood before me obediently awaiting her next command. I left hold of my hardened manhood and stepped towards her. I reached my hands behind her head and unlocked the gag that had imprisoned her lips and slowly removed it, tossing it on the bed for later use.

I did not think of myself as a cruel man and I normally treated my slave girls with kindness and consideration for their underlying humanity. But, I have to confess, the temptations of nearly omnipotent powers over the imbonded females of the resort had taught me the pleasures of the arbitrary exercise of authority. Mary had spoken once out of turn the first night that she had arrived, a product of her fear of abuse from the strange, scar faced, evil looking man to whom she had been delivered. I had rebuked her with five strokes of a riding crop and since then had imposed a rule that she be consistently gagged at all times when her delectable lips and mouth were not desired for use or for other utilitarian purposes such as eating or hygiene. I don't think that I had heard her utter more than a hundred words in the several months since she had become my adoring plaything. I have to grant her that she seemed to accept my draconian remedy to her singular outburst with grace. I had never detected any hint of resentment or protestation. I had made sure that the rule was strictly enforced even when she was away from me and it must have been a terrible burden not to be able to communicate with anyone, not even her fellow slave girls, since that night. I didn't know anything of her prior life or what she had been like before her captivity, but her enforced silence seemed to suit her brooding, dark personality as I knew it.

The black haired beauty smiled at the freedom granted to her lips and stretched and licked them as if to reacquire a familiarity with them. I was overcome with desire for her. I reached my arms around her slender torso and pulled her to me, taking possession of her lips with mine and exploring her mouth with my tongue. She gave a soft sigh as I possessed her, mingling her hot tongue with mine and wrapping her arms around me in reciprocation of my lust. Her soft body pressed against mine and her pleasant, round breasts were crushed against my chest. I could feel her hardened nipples indenting my skin and her body writhed slightly, electrifying my skin at our points of contact.

My heart went out to this unfortunate girl who had borne so much and who exhibited such pleasure and delight at my presence. I was her lord, her protector and she had apparently exchanged any resentment of my treatment of her for the slight security I could provide her and the minor kindnesses I had shown.

For some reason, out of all the nights that I had possessed her flesh, of all the times that I had used her body for my pleasure, this night I became overwhelmed with affection and need for her loving embrace. I edged our bodies to the bed and I gently guided her onto it. The bed was wide enough to accommodate the three of us easily during our many impassioned fuck fests and I was able to lie her down across the bed width wise.

I wanted Carol to have a clear, untrammeled view of our lovemaking, and before I sank my body down onto the expectant, luxurious flesh that awaited me, I glanced up at her. Her lips were still sealed by the leather shield that was stretched across them and her wrists were affixed tightly behind her back, making her heavy, round breasts jut out at attention. I could see the developing lust in her eyes and dismay at the tantalizing image of me mounting her sister slave's body. Before returning my attentions to the delectable femininity below me, I reached out my hand and stroked the hairless nexus between her forcibly outstretched thighs until I sensed the heightening of her arousal. When I withdrew my hand from her quim, she gave a little squeak of protest and I could see her hips press forward, seeking to resume the lost contact.

But my full attention was soon drawn back to the luscious, impassioned female beneath me. I was kneeling between her outstretched thighs and she had pressed them against mine as a not too subtle reminder of the need that I had generated in her by my promise of a proper fucking. I lowered myself on to her and resumed my exploration of her hot mouth with my tongue as I reveled in the softness of her body and the heat of her skin against mine. My cock was pressed firmly against her taut belly. Her soft, delicate hands were on my shoulders and she drew my body tightly against hers. I placed my hands on the sides of her head, stroking her glossy, dark black hair as I drew heat and passion from her mouth. Mary gave a little moan and I could feel her hips shifting under me expectantly, grinding my cock against her tummy urging me to a fuller possession of her.

I slowly raised my hips to free my cock from between us and I felt the slave girl's hand encircle my meat, pulling it down towards her needy crevasse. She dragged its bulbous head along the length of her fevered slit twice, giving me a tantalizing portent of the pleasure that awaited me inside. When the helmet of my cock was poised still at the entrance to her gate, she gave it a little, gentle tug and I obediently pressed my hips forward until I could feel my heated tool descend into her luscious, hot canal.

We groaned in unison as my thick meat pressed aside the walls of her pussy and entered her. I sank myself into her fully, letting the delight of the encompassment of my swollen cock send waves of pleasure throughout my body. The lustful slave girl had spread her thighs widely and her heels had found purchase on the backs of my thighs, pressing me deeper and deeper within her. I began to rock my hips gently, reveling in the feel of her velvety interior as I scraped my cock along it.

I was overwhelmed with the desire to watch the face of my partner in coitus as I plowed her furrow, driving her passions higher and higher. I raised my head and separated our lips. Her starry blue eyes peered back at me intently as I sawed my cock back and forth within her. Her plush lips were parted and I could hear the panting of her breath as her body recorded my long, slow, languorous strokes of her cunt. I could feel her body's urgency, her desire for completion, for a manic thrusting of my meat inside her. But I wanted the pleasure of possessing her flesh to last, to extend the delightful sensations as long as possible. And I wanted to drive the impassioned female who had deserved so much better in her life, had been deprived of so much, to repeated explosions of lust.

I could feel Mary's body begin to tremor and squirm beneath me as she approached her first climax. Her hands were gripping my upper arms like she was holding on for dear life and her feet and legs slid up and down the back of mine excitedly. She began to moan and she closed her pretty blue eyes as her pussy began to pulse and spasm around my enflamed meat. Her back arched and her face cringed as her orgasm hit her. "Ohhhhhhhh! Ohhhhhhhhh!" she moaned. She clenched my body tightly and was trying to thrust her hips back at me to quicken the pace of my strokes. But I held her pinioned with my own hips, pinning her to the soft mattress beneath her. I was in control of her orgasms, her lust, and I was determined that she would not exhaust her passion on her first go round.

When her shuddering subsided, I caressed her fevered face with one hand, balancing myself with the other, as I continued my steady, long, leisurely strokes within her. Her eyes opened as she realized that her exquisite torture was to continue. Her tongue licked her reddened, lust filled lips and she took a deep breath, exhaling her air with a low, deep sigh. Her legs released mine and she dug her heels deeply into the mattress, pushing her loins against me. Her thighs pressed against my hips and then released them as her eyes fluttered and she gave herself over to another bout of ecstasy.

I watched her tense face, blushed with the effects of her lust, record each contraction of her excited crevasse. I sighed with pleasure as I felt each clasp of her pussy's walls along the length of my tool. My lust was growing higher and higher, but I was determined not to come, not until I brought her to one more explosive, pleasure giving climax.

As her orgasm receded, I slowed my hips' thrusts against hers until my motions had come to a halt. She was breathing heavily, her chest rising and falling and her breasts quivering with each deep intake and outtake of air. Leaving my hard and ready tool to lie inside her momentarily at rest, I leaned down and took her right teat in my mouth and gave it a gentle suck, running my tongue over its tip. The girl moaned appreciatively and I could feel her pussy give a twitch as it received the pleasurable message from above. Dragging my tongue across her chest, I took her other nipple between my lips and, after giving it a long, soothing suckle, increased the pressure of my efforts until the lust filled slave girl moaned and gave a little cry of pleasure.

I was ready now to begin the final act in our performance for the frustrated and moaning Carol, who I knew was watching us with envy and dismay. I gathered Mary's long, soft arms in my hands and brought them over her head, pinning her wrists against the mattress. I let my chest fall back down on hers, pressing her full, soft breasts down against her and then took her wet, soft lips and thrust my tongue between them. Lost in her lust, Mary squirmed her body beneath mine, struggling to free her imprisoned hands as she reciprocated my tongue's exploration of her hot mouth. She groaned loudly from deep within her throat and I could feel her hips press against mine, desperate for a resumption of my motion within her.

I began to rock my hips slowly, almost imperceptivity at first, and then began to gradually increase the speed and intensity. I wanted to spill myself inside the hot hole that was wrapped around my cock. As my thrusts gained speed, the girl struggled to meet them. As my need grew higher and higher, I lost any pretense at control of my lust and gave out an agonized groan at each deep, intensely pleasurable penetration. The black haired slave girl began to cry and moan as her third orgasm approached. Our lips parted and I heard her voice cry out "Oh yes! Oh yes, Master! Oh yes, Master! Oh! Oh! Oh!" as she came. My cock exploded inside her and I growled at each fierce convulsion of my manhood. My brain was overwhelmed with the messages of pleasure that shot through me. My fluid poured out into her in a series of body wrenching ejaculations that seemed like they would never stop.

But, eventually, stop they did. As I felt the last, weak echo of my orgasm throb along my cock, I let out a long, deep sigh and collapsed on top of the panting, moaning girl.

I released her hands and she encircled my body with them, gripping me tightly as her legs circled my thighs and held me fast within her.

"Oh, master!" she sighed. "Thank you, master, thank you! That was wonderful! Thank you, master!"

I raised my head and was startled to see tears flowing down her cheeks. She was overcome with emotion.

"I'm sorry for speaking, master, but I couldn't hold it back. I love you, master, I love you. Please don't ever let me go. Please! Please!"

I felt a surge of affection for the poor, enslaved young woman. I stroked her head, calming her. "I'll never send you away, Mary," I answered. But deep inside me I felt a swelling up of sorrow. I would never send her away, it was true. But what would I do when Rukimo or Klitzman or somebody else tried to take her away from me? What would I do then?

We lay in each others arms for a long while. My cock had softened and I felt it slip from inside her. As I lay there I wondered whether I was wrong in giving her my affection and treating her with kindness. I was giving her false hope, I knew that. It was a terrible deception, I knew that deep inside me. But what was I to do? I could not bring myself to treat my loving slave girls harshly. Wasn't it better to allow them at least this temporary haven against the cruel fate that had befallen them? Would the happiness they felt at being my pets assuage at least a little bit the harshness and misery which would inevitably follow? I didn't know. Somehow, though, against all logic and probability, I believed that I would be able to save them.

At long last, I recovered the energy to raise my body from the still sighing and happy slave girl. I remembered the trussed and gagged slave girl at the foot of the bed. Carol was staring at me with her large, moist brown eyes. I rose from the bed and released her ankles from their confinements and then freed her wrists from behind her back. After I had released the gag from her mouth, she turned to me and leapt into my arms. "Oh, master," she cried, "that was so nice! I love you too, master! Keep me too, master! Please keep me too!"

She gripped her arms around me tightly and pressed her flesh against me. "You can do anything you want to me, master! Anything! But please don't ever send me away, please!"

I hugged the crying slave girl close to my body and kissed her on the neck. "I won't ever send you away, Carol. You belong to me. I'll never send you away, I promise."

I let the chestnut haired slave girl expend her emotions against me. Mary had risen to her knees on the bed and was smiling warmly at the display of affection from her sister slave and companion. Although my forces were expended, I decided that Carol deserved a reward for her expression of devotion.

"Mary," I said. "Don't you think that Carol deserves something for having to watch you fuck?"

The black haired girl nodded agreeably. I led Carol to the bed and Mary took hold of her arm and pulled her towards her. Their bodies and mouths joined and they fell to the mattress in an impassioned embrace. Carol parted their lips for a moment and called out to her friend, "I love you too, Mary! I do! I love you!"

Mary silently took repossession of the impassioned girl's lips and resumed their lustful embrace.

I watched as the obviously infatuated girls expressed themselves with their bodies and their caresses. There was a bottle of single malt scotch on my dresser and I took the opportunity to pour myself a few inches. There was an easy chair in the corner of the room and I pulled it up to the bed and sat in it.

For the next twenty minutes, the two slave girls kissed and caressed each other passionately. I watched intently as they fed on each other's lips and stroked each other's quims, suckled each others breasts. Their bodies writhed against each others, shifting positions several times. There was no pretense or pretend in their passions for each other. Their caresses were gentle and loving. When Carol came for the first time, I could see Mary's evident happiness at giving her sister slave pleasure. When her tremors were done, Carol gratefully pushed her lover to her back and delved between her thighs with her lips until Mary was panting and moaning and had been granted her own exquisite relief.

I had finished my scotch and my cock had begun to stir at the sight of the beautiful, young female bodies engrossed in such loving, prolonged sexual abandon. I'm no sexual Hercules but I was ready for another bout. I wanted to sink my flesh in Carol's body, it was her turn after all, and I climbed back on the bed. The girls turned to me with delight in their eyes and pulled me towards them. I joined my body to theirs and let the heat of their skin excite me as we all explored each other with our lips and hands. When my manhood had resumed its battle readiness, I pushed Carol to her knees and had her bend over. "Mary," I said, "get between Carols' legs and put your mouth on her pussy. I'm going to fuck her in the ass."

Mary smiled and snaked herself between Carol's widespread thighs. Carol obediently raised her hips to give her lover access to her pudenda. I waited until I heard her give out a prolonged sigh of pleasure, signaling the commencement of Mary's attentions to her loins and then presented my hardened cock to her little brown star.

As I pushed my cock's head into the small entrance, Carol relaxed herself to receive me. "Oh, yes, master," she sighed as I slowly entered her. "Oh God, yes," she sighed again as I felt the tight ring of flesh expand and admit me.

Although Mary enjoyed my use of her rear and responded passionately to ass fucking, Carol really loved it. I was sure that getting fucked in the ass was the farthest thing from her mind when she was still a free, young, innocent woman. She had still been a virgin when she was kidnapped, but now she reveled in my salacious use of her body, especially the narrow, but flexible hole of her rear. I felt her anus grip tightly against me as I began my strokes. I circled my hands around her torso and took possession of her wonderful, soft, firm pillows of flesh and squeezed them until she gave out a long moan of pleasure. "Ohhhhhhhhhhhh, yes, master. Yessssssss! Oh, yessssssss!"

In spite of my prior sexual expenditures, the excitement of Carol's exclamations and the warmth of her electrified flesh drove me quickly along the road to orgasm. Carol's exclamations were getting louder and louder and more frequent as the dual efforts of her lovers, Mary at her pussy, me at her ass, drove her lusts higher and higher. Suddenly, her body began to shudder and she cried out loudly. I could feel the pulsing of her cunt as it echoed in her rectum and my cock started to spurt and jerk within her. I gave a loud, happy groan and pounded my hips against her plump rear globes as I came. It was quick, but intense and, when my ejaculations slowed, I let my body collapse on the slave girl's curved, bent over back. I was done for the night.

CHAPTER THREE

It took a few minutes for the three of us to regain our energies and part our flesh. Mary continued to give Carol's pussy slow, languid licks and the echoes of Carol's winding down contractions in her passage of pleasure reverberated on my detumescing cock. I eventually slid off of Carol's back and fell to the mattress. I sensed the girls separating and while Carol snuggled up against me, Mary ran into the bathroom and returned with a bowl of water and a soapy washcloth for the cleaning of my tool. The washcloth was warm and I gave a little sigh of pleasure when she wrapped my softened Johnson in it. She rinsed the cloth in the bowl several times, making sure that my cock was clean of soap before taking the cloth and bowl back to the bathroom. When she returned, she lay on the other side of me and nestled under my outstretched arm.

The storm outside was still raging and I could hear the rain drumming on the windows and, occasionally, the rolling clap of a mighty peel of thunder. Mary had turned out the light before she returned to bed and every once in a while, the room was brightened by a flash of lightning, illuminating our naked and exhausted bodies on the bed. My mind was racing with the exhilaration of our prolonged, emotional bout of pleasure together. I tried to imagine what I had ever done to deserve such bliss. I knew it was a false paradise. The girls would surely have chosen freedom instantly if given the option over bondage to me. But part of me wanted to think that in the unlikely event the girls ever regained their freedom they would look back on their time with me with some affection.

It took a while for me to go to sleep. My two lovelies were breathing deeply in their own contentedness. And why not? They had escaped another day of brutality and indifferent exploitation on the island, something few, if any, of the other girls could claim. They hadn't been forced to fuck strange men, giving in to their most scurrilous and base demands, they hadn't been whipped. And they had been shown some kindness and consideration for their needs. While the girls slept the sleep of the innocent, my mind continued to race through the various forces which made our idyllic co-existence precarious. The storm outside seemed symbolic of the danger that threatened our little, strange family as the wind rattled the windows of my little cottage and the loud, explosive collision of nature's energies echoed throughout.

I am sad to say that that was the last night that the three of us spent together. I fell asleep ignorant of the terrible events that the next day would bring us.

* * * * * * * * * * * * * *

I awoke, as I did almost every morning, to the sensation of a pair of loving lips stroking my morning hard-on. Carol was still lying next to me, her breath steady and slow, fast asleep, and so I knew that it was Mary getting the jump on her companion in servitude in giving me my morning pleasure.

I raised my head slightly until I could see the bobbing black hair covered head at my loins. I smiled and lay my head back down, letting the moist heat of the slave girl's mouth draw my juices into my cock. I must have groaned unconsciously with pleasure because I felt Carol stirring next to me. She looked down and, seeing Mary busily at work, gave a little squeal. I took hold of her long, chestnut colored braid at the back of her head and drew her lips to mine. When I came, I moaned my pleasure into her mouth.

When she knew that my climax was finished, Carol broke our kiss and jumped up to her knees. The girls often competed for the right to take my discharge in their mouths and had worked out an equitable resolution of their competing desires. Mary's head rose from my loins and I saw her with a sardonic, pleased smile on her face. She rose to her knees and joined her lips to Carol's. My cum was pooled on her tongue and she let the other slave girl slurp a fair portion of it out of her mouth with hers. When they had finished exchanging my spunk, they turned to me, smiled and swallowed their respective shares.

It was a little after 6:30 and it was time for my run. I usually put in a five miler every morning. It kept me in shape and helped work off the effects of my high living. I left my girls' ankles locked to a ring in the slave's bathroom so that they could pee and wash up. I unloaded my bladder of water and then stepped outside.

The rain had stopped during the night and the air was fresh and clean. I circled around the edges of the resort and took my turn through the golf course. The run was invigorating but uneventful and when I returned to my cottage I released my slave girls from their chains and took my shower.

I let Mary wash me while Carol prepared my breakfast. Since she had had the benefit of my cock already this morning, I gently declined her offer of another oral release even though her caresses of my flesh while soaping and rinsing me had driven my cock to hardness.

I had just finished eating the buttered toast that Carol had prepared for me and was downing the remnants of the coffee she had brewed when the telephone rang. The girls were kneeling next to each other on either side of my chair. I had been feeding them small bits of melon from the fruit salad that Carol had put together. Slave girls were certainly not allowed to handle knives and the bits of fruit had been sent up the night before and placed in the small refrigerator which served my cottage. Carol had merely mixed the fruit and poured juice over it. The three of us looked ominously over at the phone. It was an unexpected intrusion into our happy, little world.

My telephone was purely an inside line and I knew that the only people who would be calling me were Rukimo or Anthony. In the past, an early morning phone call had presaged a call to special duty and so I was filled with some trepidation when I stepped across the room and answered it. It was Anthony.

"Morning Harry," he said. "Did I wake you?"

"No," I answered. "I've been up for a while. What can I do for you?"

"Mr. K wants you to report to his place right away."

I wondered what Klitzman could want so early in the morning. The idea that he would be up so early was strange. But then, maybe he never went to bed. He spent all his time in his luxurious mansion with his bevy of private slave stock. Night and day probably had no meaning for him.

"Sure," I answered. "I'll come right now."

"And bring that slave girl, Mary, with you," Anthony added. I felt a lump form in my chest. What could Klitzman want with Mary? Was this the day that I had been fearing for so long?"

"How come?" I asked with some trepidation.

"Never mind, how come," Anthony answered annoyance in his voice. "Just do what the fuck you're told, Harry. Got it?"

"Okay, okay" I replied. Anthony rang off.

I held the telephone receiver in my hand for a long minute while I tried to process the orders that I had been given. What would Klitzman want with Mary? He had access to any one of a hundred and fifty girls at any time and first crack at any newly acquired lovelies. What made Mary so special to him? Whatever it was, it couldn't be good.

Mary and Carol were looking at me expectantly when I turned back to them after returning the receiver to the hook. My unhappiness must have been clear on my face.

"What's the matter, master?" Carol asked. I didn't know how to answer her. What could I do? To refuse was unthinkable. Short of throwing Mary off the cliff next to my cottage, she was going to Klitzman's. Maybe that's what I should do, I thought. Being under the thumb of Klitzman was indeed a fate worse than death, as Carol had discovered to her own dismay. Would she be better off dead? And maybe I should join her in the plunge. I couldn't bear the thought of the abuse she would undoubtedly suffer at the cruel man's hands.

But, on the other hand, maybe I could talk him out of it. Maybe I could ask him a favor. I had done a great deed for him a few weeks ago in helping to complete one of his missions on the mainland. Didn't he owe me something?

We can think ourselves into anything. Any rational person would not have given a tinker's chance that Mary wasn't going to be taken away from me, that some dim, unfortunate future was beckoning for her. But I knew that I couldn't bring myself to kill her or myself for that matter. I was a coward, I admit it. I wanted to live. I didn't want to face my maker just yet. And so I grabbed at the slight wisp of a chance that I could alter Mary's fate. I was wrong. Dead wrong.

"Nothing's the matter," I barked back at Carol, annoyed that she had interposed her concern into my own. "I've got to go somewhere. Get up and put your shoes on and get your gags."

I could see the look of unhappiness on the girls' faces. They knew something was up. They stayed in place for a moment absorbing the fear and unhappiness exuding from my face. They looked so vulnerable in their nudity, the accouterments of confinement affixed on their bodies, symbols and tools of their enslavement. "Get up and get going!" I yelled, pissed that they were making this harder for me. "Or do you both need a whipping?"

The girls jumped to their feet and ran into the slave alcove to put on their red high heeled shoes. They then dashed into the bedroom and retrieved their gags. They hustled back into the living area and stood forlornly in front of me. I quickly took their gags from their hands and pushed them roughly into their mouths. I didn't want any more questions. Their eyes were tear filled as I ordered them to turn around so that I could bind their wrists behind their backs. I left them standing there facing the wall while I went to the bedroom and put on a fresh reddish brown robe, my uniform as a supervisor on the island, and a pair of sandals. I tied the robe tightly around my midsection and went out to where the slave girls were waiting.

I stood behind them for a moment, hesitant to begin the journey that might lead to Mary's doom. Their pinioned hands were writhing nervously behind them. Carol's braided, chestnut hair descended down her back, the tip brushing against her joined wrists. Mary's black hair sat resting on her shoulders and down to the top of her spine. Their bright red high heels made them seem taller and set their posture at attention. Two helpless slave girls. I looked at the matching, bright red, cursive "*k*"'s burned and dyed into their rear cheeks denoting their loss of human rights. How painful it must have been, I thought, how dismal the experience of being converted from free women to sexual chattel. How pathetic was the hope that they had placed in me to be their protector.

"Turn around," I ordered them curtly. Tears were flowing down their faces. They knew that there was something terribly wrong. For a moment I contemplated hooding them so that I would not have to see their unhappy expressions. But I thought better of it. I would not add to their misery and fear. I took the two leashes that I kept handy and affixed the ends to their collars. I gave them a hard tug and pulled them behind me out of the cottage.

It was a five minute walk to the Slave center where the girls would ordinarily spend their days. I had the girls' leashes gripped tightly in my right hand and I could hear the clip clopping of their shoes on the brick pathway behind me as we walked. I could see their frightened eyes and unhappy faces in my mind as we went along. Usually, I made this traverse light heartedly, the vision of another day in paradise in my head. But today, my heart was heavy with grief and worry. I wanted to get it over with as quickly as possible and so our pace was about double our usually pleasant, leisurely stroll.

When we reached the entrance to the Slave Center, a little hut that housed the elevator to the underground facility, I stopped and waited for the car to reach the surface. It seemed an eternity before the sliver door opened. Three pretty, naked slave girls, gagged and bound and strung together in a coffle, emerged and quickly stepped out to dash to their destination. Mary and Carol moved to enter the elevator car. I held Mary back and released

Carol's leash. The dismally unhappy, brown haired girl turned and looked back at me.

"Get in!" I yelled at her. I heard her give a great sob and she turned and stepped into the empty car. She turned back again to look at me. The tears were flowing down her face in a stream. The leash that I had been holding dangled from her collar down between her heaving breasts. Her face was frantic with dismay. Slowly, inexorably, the door closed.

Mary was standing next to me, sobbing heavily. I could see her reflection in the shiny steel of the elevator door. Her eyes were peering at me helplessly, hoping for some sign from me that would provide a benign explanation for the unusual turn of events. She clearly understood the import of not being allowed to enter the elevator. Whatever was wrong involved her. Turning away from her piteous, reflected visage, I gave her leash a harsh tug and started the journey to her fate.

Klitzman's mansion was at the far edge of the pleasure complex. I had been there a number of times to receive his instructions or to, I suppose, amuse him with my company. The large fenced gate that regulated entrance into Klitzman's domain was manned by a pair of the tall, muscular, black robed guards who enforced discipline on the island. I was expected and they waived me through. A walkway paved with multicolored slabs of slate about 50' long led up to the actual door to the mansion. As I walked along it, my heart was pounding and my stomach was turning. I had to do something. I couldn't let them take Mary away. I stopped before the massive, wooden doors that barred admission into and out of the mansion. They were ornately caved with a host of miniature scenes of sexual depravity, a very accurate representation of what took place inside. Girls who were drafted into Klitzman's personal hell often never came back, too damaged physically or mentally to be used in the resort proper. If I couldn't convince the behemoth glutton to forgo this particular morsel, would Mary be one of the lucky ones? Would I ever see her again?

Mary's sobbing had subsided and I turned to look at her. Her breasts were quivering and her nipples were hardened with fear. Sweat was running down her chest and from under her arms. Her high heels clicked nervously on the brick pathway as we hesitated before the gates of hell. In spite of her dismay, she was a vision of delight. I ran my eyes over her flesh, her firm, round, pleasant breasts, the way that her taut belly sloped and narrowed down to her delicate, hairless love lips, her graceful, trim thighs, her round, delicious hips. Anyone would want her, that was clear. But I wanted her more than anything I had ever wanted. I didn't want to lose her. Her happy, impassioned mien from the night before sprang into my mind. What a difference a few hours could make.

She was whining softly, probably unconsciously. I wanted to speak to her, to assuage her torment, to assure her that nothing bad was going to happen, but I knew that it would be a lie. Turning away from her forlorn, unhappy, fear filled eyes, I pressed the buzzer for admittance.

The door was opened by one of Klitzman's guards. His black face was hard and shiny, expressionless. His muscles bulged from beneath his tight, black robe. On his belt he wore one of the long, black, electrified batons that served as the standard weapon of the island's police force. He stood by and let us pass.

I dragged the reluctant Mary along the green and black mottled, marble floor and headed to where I suspected I would find the demonic commander of this perverse resort. His reception room stood off to the right side of the entrance about 20' in and was separated from the tall ceilinged hallway by a large archway. As I stepped down into the vast, cathedral like room, I saw Klitzman seated at his ordinary perch, in the middle of a large circular couch. He was wearing his plush, bright red robe which was striped with thin golden threads. His flesh flowed around it and his pudgy face was encircled by a layer of fat, offset by his close cropped, sparse, reddish grey hair. His gigantic thighs were spread and, as usual, a slender, naked slave girl was ensconced between them, his fleshy weapon in her mouth. To his left, sitting in an easy chair, was a tall but slightly built Asian man, dressed in sharply creased black slacks and a loose, multicolored, flowered, buttonless shirt. His features were sharp and cruel looking. When I pulled poor Mary into the room behind me, his eyes lit up and he smiled. He stood to greet us.

"Harry!" Klitzman roared. "Good to see ya!" Klitzman was a madman, there was no doubt of that. He thought it clever to disguise his voice in various accents as he spoke with you, assuming the intonations of BBC English, an Australian twang, an American Southern drawl. Today he seemed to have assumed the demeanor of a Midwestern farmer. I tried to disguise my nervousness as I replied.

"It's always good to see you, Mr. Klitzman," I lied. It was actually never good to see him.

Klitzman rudely shoved the slave girl who had been servicing him aside. I didn't need to see his fat, rampant, reddened cock spring from her mouth. There were about six or seven other slave girls kneeling in a semicircle about fifteen feet away from Klitzman's couch, their foreheads married to the smooth marble floor in front of them. Their wrists were crossed behind their backs. Most of them exhibited some evidence of abuse or another, long, red lash marks, splotches of black and blue, angry, red lacerations to their skin. The discarded slave girl scurried to join them.

When she had assumed her position, Klitzman resumed the conversation, such as it was.

"I see ya brought the black haired slut with you, Harry. You had her so long I thought you were going to marry her!" Klitzman's voice was deep and loud. It echoed through the large room. He had a shit eating grin across his face. He laughed loudly and coarsely at his idea of a joke.

I had taken hold of Mary's leash just below her chin and was holding her fast. I could sense her trembling body next to me. She was slightly behind me to my right and had not yet seen the Asian man.

"Is her cunt made of gold, Harry? Or maybe it tastes like ice cream, huh? Everybody seems to want it."

Mary took a step forward to get a look at the man to my left. I heard her gasp and emit a loud, forlorn sob. I looked over at her. Her face was etched with intense terror. She tried to pull way from me and I saw her body sag as her knees weakened. What was this all about?

And then it struck me. Carol had told me the tale of Mary's abuse at the hands of a Cambodian colonel, a man who had tormented and practically broken her body soon after she had been released from training and brought to the Slave Center. He had promised to come back and buy her when he had made enough money from the heroin smuggling operation he and his general ran from the jungles of that unhappy country. I had thought it an empty boast. Why would he pick Mary when he had so many other girls to choose from? But here he was. This was worse than I thought.

"Let me introduce Colonel Huong, Harry," Klitzman intoned. "He's got a dang awful hankering for your little slave girl there. I'm sure that ya will compliment him on his good taste, eh?"

I was speechless. This was the worse thing that could have happened. This man was going to take Mary back to the jungles of Cambodia to a life of daily torture and pain. I would never see her again.

"I am happy to meet you, Harry," the Asian said, his voice sharp and formal. "Mr. Klitzman has told me all about you."

I tried to respond with a polite, formal response, but a cat had my tongue.

Huong turned to Klitzman. "She is just as I remember her. I am grateful that you have kept her secured for me."

Huong's statement was like a kick in the teeth. That was why Mary had been sent to me and why I had been able to keep her for so long. I was keeping her from the hazards of the resort for the benefit of this cruel Asian. I was a dupe, a pawn. I felt a wall of anger rise up inside me.

The slightly built Asian stepped forward closer to his prey. Mary was sobbing again. She tried to shy away as the man approached. He took the leash from my hand and drew her body up to him. For some reason, maybe because of my shock, I let the leash slide from my grip.

"I have been thinking of you often, my dear." Huong said to the distressed, abysmally fearful girl. He took a hand and placed it atop Mary's left breast. His hand covered it and he pressed his fingers in against her soft, bulging flesh, seemingly looking for a particular point of sensitivity. When he found it, he squeezed it harshly.

Mary's legs gave out and she sank to her knees. She released a howl of pain and misery. It was as if the Asian knew precisely the point where squeezing her breast would bring her the most anguish. The man looked at her with an intense coldness. He was studying her reaction as if he had been acting to reaffirm her responsiveness. He released her breast and smiled, turning back to the cruel, corrupt ruler of this devilish domain.

"As I remembered," he said, his voice polite and pleasant. "I will take her with me today."

Suddenly I found my voice. "No you won't," I roared. "Keep your fucking hands off of her."

Huong looked at me with surprise. "You object?" he asked, incredulous. "Why would anyone care about a slave girl?" his expression said. He pulled Mary to her feet by her leash. Mary was still moaning with pain and his action propelled her into a fit of hysteria. She had heard him when he said he was going to take her.

"Leeeeeeeeeas! Ooooooooo! Oooooooooo! Leeeeease!" she screamed from behind her gag. She frantically tried to turn away from the man, but he held her leash tightly. His grin spread across his face. It was just the reaction that he desired. He turned back to me.

"But she's mine. I bought her," he said calmly. "I can do anything I want to her." He had brought Mary back to her feet and he slid his free hand between her thighs and took hold of her hairless nether lips. He gave them a harsh, cruel squeeze. Mary's howls renewed with an ever more intense fury. Her eyes were opened widely in terror. It was too much to watch.

A cloud of red flowed over my eyes. I leapt at the slender Asian man with the intent of breaking his neck. I got to about a foot away from him and he turned and shot his hand out at me, catching me full in the chest. To my surprise my body flew back about ten feet and I fell to the floor. My chest felt like someone had hit it with a sledgehammer. All at once I saw the finely sculpted muscles under the man's shirt. He looked at me with a calmness that belied the blow that he had just given me.

I rose quickly to my feet. "Harry!" Klitzman yelled out, "Stop!"

I knew that I could not handle the cruel Asian man to man. There was a large wrought iron lamp on the table near where I had fallen. I grabbed it and yanked the plug from the wall. Out of the corner of my eye I saw one of Klitzman's African guards rushing up behind me. Heedless, I moved towards the Asian, the lamp lifted over my head. I was going to crush his skull. Suddenly, I felt a fierce jolt enter my body from my back just over my shoulder blade. There was a loud 'crack!' and my body stiffened. The guard had zapped me with his baton. I paused for a moment, the lamp hovering over my head. I saw Mary's unhappy eyes peering at me, her face awash with tears. I took another halting step forward, determined to destroy the Asian. Another, fiercer jolt ran through my body. I felt my eyes roll back and my legs gave out underneath me. I passed out before I hit the floor, my love object's anguished face was the last thing that I saw.

* * * * * * * * * * * * * *

When I awoke, I was sitting on a hard concrete floor. It took a few moments for me to come to full awareness. My whole body ached. I tried to recall how I had ended up here. My robe had been taken from my body and I was naked. My wrists were locked into a thick leather belt that was wrapped around my waist. One dim light bulb lit the room from the middle of the low, concrete, whitewashed ceiling. The room was small, about 10' by 8'. There was no furnishings except for a thin cotton pallet and a stainless steel pail, no interruptions to the sea of faded white concrete that surrounded me but a small ventilator opening low in the wall opposite. "What the fuck?" I thought.

Then I remembered. Mary was gone. Gone to a life of misery and torment. I had failed her. I hadn't cried since I was a boy, but at that moment my eyes filled up with tears and I broke into heavy, body wrenching sobs. My whole body shook with the effects of my uncontrolled weeping. I curled my body into a ball and crawled into the corner of the room. I had never been so dismal in my life. How could I have let it happen? Why couldn't I save her? What kind of person was I?

My bawling continued for what must have been the better part of an hour. I would stop and regain my composure and then I would begin all over again. I was exhausted physically and emotionally when I was finished. I lay there for a long time trying to drive my misery out of my head.

I realized that I must be in one of Klitzman's dungeons. That didn't bother me. It was where I felt that I belonged. Not only had I failed Mary, but I had failed Carol too. I would be killed, I had no doubt of that, and she would suffer a fate not too dissimilar in one way or another from Mary's. By trying to save one, I had lost them both. And any hopes I had had of bringing down Klitzman's empire was irreparably lost.

I don't know how long it was before I heard the lock on the heavy wooden door that led to my cell open. I rose from the floor to a sitting position, ready to receive my deathblow with some dignity. One of the African guards swung the door open and a tall, lanky, naked slave girl with thick, shoulder length, straw colored hair entered carrying a small metal tray. The guard closed the door behind her. Apparently my ultimate fate was to be delayed. The tray held a bowl of some kind of stew and a tall, plastic cup of water. She set the bowl down next to me and knelt on the floor. There was a large spoon buried in the stew and she picked it up and brought a spoonful of the dark, brown mixture to my lips.

Eating was the last thing I wanted to do. I turned my head from her and stared at the empty wall. She put down the spoon and brought the cup to my lips. I clasped my lips tightly refusing it.

The girl knelt back and put the cup back down on the tray. She picked up the tray and silently went back to the door. Holding the tray in one hand, she knocked on the door with the other. A minute or so later, the door opened and she was let out.

I would like to tell you that I maintained my principled resolve to starve myself to death in sorrow and shame, but I didn't. The third time that a slave girl brought me a tray of food, I let her feed me. I was hungry and my stomach was aching with cramps. My throat was parched. Well, I decided, maybe I'll get a chance to spit in Klitzman's face before I die. I'll keep my strength up for that, I thought.

Once I had eaten and drank the water, the girl knocked on the door and left. She hadn't said a word to me and I hadn't said a word to her. A few moments later, she came back with a large bowl of steaming water and a washcloth.

I don't know how long I had been a prisoner, but I had really begun to stink. I had used the pail a couple of times to dispose of my wastes, but since my hands were fastened to my sides and there was no toilet paper anyway, I had been unable to wipe myself. My spirits had revived somewhat from the food and I figured that I might as well die clean.

I stood in the middle of the room and let the slave girl wash my body. She had long, loose, straight, brown hair with darkly hued skin, small but plump breasts and wide, sexy hips. Her hands flowed around my body gently and expertly. God forgive me, but the sensation of her rubbing my body, fondling and cleaning my cock and balls, running her hands over my ass and legs, brought my manhood to an embarrassing attention. This is what got me into trouble in the first place. When she finished, she sank to her knees in front of me and took possession of my rampant cock in her hands. She pressed her face forward and opened her mouth to subsume my prick. But enough was enough. A guy has to have some standards after all. I was in mourning for Mary and Carol and it just didn't seem right that my libido had been stoked by the handling of my flesh.

I backed away from the girl and told her "No." She looked up at me, surprised, shrugged her shoulders and rose from the floor. She took the bowl to the door, knocked on it and was let out.

I had been in prison before. Being locked up was nothing new to me. But this was solitary confinement. The blank, silent walls surrounded me. I could think of nothing except for the fate of my two girls. I knew Mary's fate and that was bad enough. But what had happened to Carol? Had Klitzman reclaimed her so that he could continue his withering torment of her body, finishing what he had started before he gave her to me? Had she been sold off the island to some scurrilous whorehouse or to some heinously cruel master? When you have nothing to do but think, the worse thoughts seem to keep coming back to your head.

I couldn't lose the picture of Mary's miserable face as she watched me go down for the count or Carol's look of dismay as the door to the Slave Center elevator closed on her. The delight that I had taken from their bodies seemed poisoned now by their fates. "Why didn't I just stay in Atlanta?" I asked myself again and again. Why did I expose myself to more misery than I had ever experienced before? Prison was safe. Emotionally dead, you kept your guard up

at all times, expected nothing from nobody and looked out
for your self. Sure, you might have buddies, but everybody
knew that everybody would sell out their mothers for a few
privileges or maybe a pack of cigarettes or even another
helping of pudding at dinner.

I had tried to keep track of time by counting the meals
that had been brought to me. I guessed that they were
giving me two meals a day. I had counted fourteen meals so
far, including the three that I had refused. That meant that
I had been locked up for seven days by my best estimate.
Of course, they could be fucking with me. The light never
went out overhead. They could be bringing me meals at
different intervals, every four hours then every six and then
maybe ten and then four again or even two. The sponge
baths I got seemed to come intermittently as did the
exchange of my soiled, steel pail for a new one. Maybe they
waited until I stunk too much and then told the slave girls
to wash me up. The only real measure of time I had was the
length of my growing beard. But there was no mirror in my
cell and so it was difficult for me to gauge how long I had
been kept a prisoner even by that inaccurate, unreliable
marker.

There seemed to be three or four different slave girls
who did duty in the dungeon. On what I calculated to be
my eighth day in captivity, the blond haired girl who had
tried to feed me the first day came in with my dinner. I was
sitting with my back against the wall as she spooned me the
muck from the bowl. She looked nervous for some reason. I
couldn't figure it out. I wasn't going to hurt her. Maybe she
knew that some evil fate was soon coming to my door and
she felt sorry for me. But why any of these girls would feel
sorry for any male who had voluntarily participated in their
abuse, no matter how 'kindly;' he had been was beyond me.

I had finished the bowl and the girl took a paper napkin and leaned over so that she could wipe my mouth. As she did so, she placed her lips next to my ear. She whispered to me in a heavily accented voice and, at first I thought that I had misunderstood her. "Carol is okay," she said.

My eyes lit up. Carol was okay? You can't imagine what joy those words brought to me. The girl continued, "She says you must live. She told me to give you something."

There was no window on the door for the guard to look through and see the girl talking to me, but I thought that there might be a hidden microphone and so I resisted interrogating the girl although my mind was roiling with questions. What was she doing? Where was she serving? How were they treating her? And what could she, a naked, abject slave girl, give me down here in my dismal cell beneath the ground that could be of any use? My last question was answered right away as the blond girl drifted her hand across my thigh and took hold of my flaccid manhood.

I moved my thigh to reject the pretty girl's advance. "No," she whispered almost desperately. "From Carol, please!"

I tried to imagine why Carol would have any concern for me. I had failed her and her sisterly lover miserably. But my heart was overwhelmed with her apparent concern for me and the memory of the two beautiful, innocent girls who had been my companions. Slowly, the blond slave girl extended her grasp again until her hand encircled my flaccid cock. The warmth of her hand sent a wave of pleasure through me. My manhood began to fill with blood as she tugged at it gently. When it had grown semi hard, the girl leaned over and placed her lips around it, taking it into her hot mouth.

The sensation of the moist heat of her mouth sent me another current of delight. I could feel my tool stiffening inside her. I reflexively opened my thighs to give her better access to me and her hand cupped my soft, wrinkled scrotal sac, caressing the delicate stones within lovingly. Her agile tongue flitted around the bulbous head of my wand bringing me a series of deliciously pleasurable sensations. My whole body relaxed for the first time since my imprisonment and I closed my eyes to better enjoy the blond haired slave's ministrations.

I thought of my beautiful Carol, her big brown eyes and her sweet smile. I recalled the two housemates laughing and giggling as they teased my body in one of our many long, delightful bouts on the big, comfortable bed in my cottage. Carol still cared for me. She had sent me a gift, the only gift that an imbonded, propertyless, sexual slave could give. Her gift had traveled through the invisible, surreptitious, haphazard grapevine that the slave girls seemed to have right down deep into the most secret and isolated portion of Klitzman's domain. And dutifully, out of an ineffable bond of sisterhood between fellow sufferers, this slave girl was delivering it.

Tears came to my eyes as I reveled in the mouth that was, in effect, Carol's, sent to me in spite of the misery and hardship that I had been ineffectual in preventing. What gift could I give her in return other than to enjoy her offering from afar, to recall her loving lips, her devotion to me? "You can do anything you want to me, master, anything. Just don't send me away," she had said. By accepting the oral caresses of her substitute, I would be confirming that she was still mine, that I still wanted her. In possessing the mouth of the blond girl, I was possessing her, occupying her body, confirming my desire for her flesh.

My lusts grew quickly under the expert oral attentions of the blond slave girl. I could feel the tell tale sensation of my rising juices, the immanency of my explosion of passion. I tried to reach my hands out to caress the luscious body of the beautiful young woman who was so exquisitely serving me, but my hands stopped short, confined by the locks on the belt around my waist. I almost laughed at the irony. Me, who had confined so many pretty, defenseless, feminine wrists prefatory to abuse, whether from me or from others, was bound and helpless to take any volitional efforts to satisfy my desires. Like a slave girl, lust was being thrust upon me and all I could do was accept it and enjoy it.

I groaned deeply when my climax began. I felt my cock throb and pulse within the blond girl's mouth, spurting my essence within her. Her oral efforts had accelerated as my passion grew and she was bobbing her head frantically over my cock, sucking intently at my jerking wand, running her hot, agile tongue around my exploding shaft. I groaned again as my climax peaked, arching my back, my muscles tense and contracted all over my body.

As my orgasm waned, my body softened and I felt a wave of satisfied comfort flow over me. I would be ready for whatever they did to me now. The thought that someone out there cared for me, remembered me with kindness and affection, was a source of joy and strength. When I was in Atlanta Federal Prison, I had not received one letter in three and a half years, not one person had come to see me. I was alone in all the world. And now, in this lowly dungeon, in one of the most cruel and heartless places on earth, someone had reached out to me to comfort me. Suddenly, I wanted to live.

CHAPTER FOUR

The blond girl visited me three more times over the next week or so. Each time she settled me back against the wall and gave me oral delight before she left. I decided that I needed to keep up my physical strength and so I started to perform a regular routine of exercise in my small cell. I walked the length of it 200 times several times a day. I did sit ups, deep knee bends and leg lifts. Several thousand every "day". I could not use my bound arms and so I concentrated on intense isometrics, pulling at my confinements with all of my might in intense, short intervals, flexing and unflexing my arm and shoulder muscles. My diet was severely limited and so I soon lost the small roll of flab that had developed over the months I had spent as a slave supervisor.

I tried to keep out of my mind what was going to happen to me. I could not help but visualize Mary in the throes of torture by the cruel Cambodian colonel who had bought her nor wonder what indignities and suffering Carol was going through. But every time I felt myself become emotionally overwhelmed at their fates, I got up and began my exercises all over again.

Finally, one day, the black robed African guard came in and motioned me with his wand to get up and leave the cell. There was no way I could fight him with my hands bound as they were and I knew that whatever fate he was summoning me to was unavoidable. I decided to go with dignity whatever it was.

I have to say that my heart was pounding and my stomach was aflutter as we mounted a series of concrete steps back up to the world. I was walking ahead of him and every time that I slowed, he gave me a little jab in the back with his baton.

We went through several large, steel doors guarded by tall, muscular, fierce looking Africans on the other side who would peer thorough the little glass window before letting us through. When we went through the last one I realized that we were back in the main part of Klitzman's mansion as I recognized the familiar green and black marble floors. We were in the hallway which led to Klitzman's reception room and I shortly found myself standing before the large, gluttonous creature.

He was sitting, as always, in the center of his large, semi-circular couch. There was a tray of food sitting in front of him and he was munching on what looked like a huge turkey leg when I came in. Two nubile slave girls were on the couch on either side of him, their legs tucked under them and their backs on the couch. Their knees were spread and they had one hand behind their heads and the other hand frigging their hairless quims between their widespread thighs. The grotesque, evil man looked up at me while he masticated a lump of meat he had torn off of the bone. Before taking his next bite, he took the turkey leg and rubbed it lengthwise against the flowing, flush pussy of the girl to his right, covering it with her moisture. He took another bite and signaled me with his head towards a chair sitting about ten feet away from him in the middle of the room.

I took a look around before I assumed the chair. There was six of Klitzman's ubiquitous stock of private slave girls kneeling by the wall to my right. Their legs were spread and their hands were joined behind their necks. Their eyes were all closed and their mouths were opened and formed into little 'o"s like they were awaiting the insertion of a cock. Their placid expressions belied the torment that I was sure they experienced every day while in Klitzman's clutches.

There was a tall, svelte woman sitting in an easy chair on the other side of the room. She was dressed all in black, a pair of tight, shiny, leather pants and a silken blouse that hugged her breasts. Her blouse was open to the beginning of her cleavage, giving a hint of the pleasant pulchritude that lay underneath. She had long, straight, black hair that went just past her shoulders. Her face was stern and sardonic looking with high, plucked, arched eyebrows, a dark, almost black lipstick and a pale complexion. She looked about 35.

Kneeling next to her, on her right, was a dainty, young girl, maybe 19 or so, with long, strait, brown hair that draped down on both sides of her pretty, pale neck down to just below her breasts. She had a thin, delicate face and her eyes were made up to give her a look of studied innocence, long, well separated lashes, a slight blush on her cheeks, pale lipstick and a light blue shadow on her eyelids. She was dressed in a prim looking white blouse with lacy frills down the front that minimized her small but plump, feminine mounds. She was wearing a pleated, pale blue and dark green, plaid skirt that touched the floor around her. She was kneeling back on her heels and her hands were joined together on her lap.

I was surprised to see two dressed females in Klitzman's domain. I wondered what fate held in store for them. The older woman was decidedly riper than the standard fare at the resort but the younger one seemed just right. The women were taking in my naked, bearded, scraggly form. I hadn't had a haircut or combed my hair in what I took to be about three weeks. My bound wrists, I was sure, bespoke some animal like nature that required confinement. And, of course, my flaccid cock was dangling loosely between my thighs. The younger woman's eyes flitted over it and then cast themselves downwards as befitted her submissive pose. The older woman's eyes took a long, hard perusal of my attributes. When finished, her eyes drifted up my rather well built form to my face. She gave me a sly, knowledgeable smile.

I sat down in the chair that Klitzman had indicated. He had swallowed the meat he had torn from the turkey bone and had picked up with his left hand a piece of bread from the tray. He leaned over to the girl on his left and swiped the bread deeply into her moist, gleaming pussy, twisting it several times to gather as much of her discharge as he could and then brought it back to his pig like face. He took an indifferent sniff of the bread and then popped into his strange, all consuming mouth.

"Harry!" he mumbled, his voice garbled by the bread, "have you had a good rest?"

His voice was high and squeaky, almost like the voice of a schoolboy whose voice was just changing. Maybe a French schoolboy. I couldn't tell.

"It has been very restful, Mr. Klitzman," I replied. "I recommend it to you some day."

Klitzman gave out a hearty laugh. Masticated bread shot out of his mouth. His huge belly shook under his bright red robe and his fleshy thighs quivered. His thighs were parted and from where I sat I could see his shrouded, greasy, fat cock lying limp between them. It was not a sight that I had wanted etched in my memory.

"Now it doesn't do to hold a grudge, Harry," he said when his laughter subsided. "You were a very bad boy."

"I thought that was why you hired me, Mr. Klitzman," I replied. "Because I was a very bad boy." I had a huge chip on my shoulder. I couldn't get out of my head that the last time I had seen Mary was in this very room and she was howling in pain. On the other hand, why tease a dinosaur? I don't know. I guess it is just my nature.

"Oh, yes, Harry!" the behemoth exclaimed. "That's right. And that's why I tolerate a little exuberance from you once in a while. But Colonel Huong is not the man to challenge to a *mano a mano*, you know what I mean?"

"I discovered that, Mr. Klitzman," I replied.

"And I can understand your infatuation with the pretty, little, black haired slave girl. Mr. Huong let me have a little fun with her before he took her away. She was quite delightful. I'm not surprised that you were disappointed to lose her."

My ire rose as the thought of the abuse that Mary must have suffered at Klitzman's hands. But I was standing on a razor's edge. I had Carol to think of. If somehow I could get back into Klitzman's good graces, maybe I could be reunited with her. Maybe this time I could think of a way to save her from Mary's fate. Maybe I could do something about bringing the evil, world class criminal down. Maybe, just maybe, I could figure out a way to save Mary, if it wasn't too late. I girded my loins, figuratively that is.

"She was a nice piece of ass, Mr. Klitzman. I had her trained the way I wanted her. I guess I kind of lost it." If I had had a forelock and my hands had been free, I would have been tugging it.

"Don't mention it, Harry. All is forgiven. Well, not quite all. I think that we'll keep you on probation for a little while until you prove your mettle again."

"Thank you, Mr. Klitzman," I said. "But what about the other one? Carol?"

"Oh, was that her name?" Klitzman replied. There was a large, beaker sized glass of wine on his tray and he had taken hold of it with his large, meaty right hand. He brought it to his fat, greasy lips and took a long pull on it. He had to lean his head back and I could see his throat convulse as he gulped it down. Not an epicure.

The fat man had paused for dramatic effect. He looked back at me and placed the glass back on the tray. The wine had left a purple moustache over his upper lip. "Well, I did give her to you," he said. "But I think that we'll hold on to her for now. She's giving delightful service in one of the guest lounges these days and I've heard some very high praise for her skills. In fact, there's been an offer on her. A very nasty, Russian fellow. He's had her for the last few days and he admires the way that she takes the whip. You could make a very nice profit."

"No thanks, Mr. Klitzman. I like to hold on to what's mine," I said trying to suppress my inner rage and anguish for Carol's fate. I'm sure that the man knew that he had gotten under my skin. Maybe there was a nasty Russian and maybe there wasn't. I tried to keep that out of my mind. I made a silent vow to kill Klitzman one day.

"We'll see, we'll see," the fat man responded. "In the meantime, I have a little job for you. I'd like you to meet Natanya Bordolinski, a very good friend of mine. She's in need of your peculiar skills and I'm going to send you on a little trip with her."

I looked over to the beautiful, black clad woman in the chair. "Pleased to make your acquaintance," I said, nodding. "I'd shake your hand, but...." I said, fluttering my hands in their confinements.

"Not at all, Harry," the woman said. Her voice was deep and sexy, with an eastern European accent. She had her hand on the head of her little friend and was playfully twirling a strand of her long, silken, chestnut colored hair as she spoke. She looked at Klitzman.

"Are you sure that Monsieur Harry is up to the travails of travel, Mr. Klitzman? He looks a little shopworn to me."

"Oh, he's up to it all right. Harry's a tough old bird and right ready with a pistol or his fists. He's smart and will do what he's told. And most of all, he's lucky. Aren't you, Harry?"

"I guess I am at that, Mr. Klitzman," I answered.

"Then it's settled. You'll leave tomorrow. We'll get Harry all duded up. He'll look like aces when you see him next. In the meantime, if you'd like to partake of one of my delectable little cunts, feel free. I've had a room prepared for you here in the mansion."

"Thank you, Mr. Klitzman, but I think Celine here needs a little discipline. And she has such a well trained tongue," the woman replied.

I could see the young girl stiffen at her mistress's intimation of an impending painful interlude. I wondered what her tale of woe was and whether she wore one of Klitzman's brands on what I presumed to be her pretty, little girl's ass.

"Suit yourself," Klitzman said reaching for another turkey leg. He mashed it against the pussy lips of the supine girl on his right and took a huge bite. "You're free to go, Harry," he mumbled through his lunch. "But don't go looking for your little slave girl. She's busy right now. Understand?"

"Understood, Mr. Klitzman," I said.

I stood and the African guard who had been looming behind me in case I decided to repeat my foolishness of a couple weeks ago stepped forward and unlocked my wrists from the belt around my waist. He then freed me from the belt. I raised and flexed my arms for the first time in two weeks. It felt good.

"And take one of my cunts with you," Klitzman continued. "That one there," he said, pointing to one of the girls along the wall with the turkey leg. It was a pleasantly shaped brunette with large, bulbous breasts. Her mounds bore the evidence of Klitzman's cruelty, several fresh, angry red stripes across them. She looked a little older than the rest, slightly worse for wear. Her hair was wavy and descended to her shoulders with cute little bangs across her forehead. Her eyes were closed and so she gave no reaction to Klitzman's designation of her as my plaything for the day.

"She's scheduled for a beating today, Harry, so make sure she gets it. I want to see her black and blue and covered with stripes when I get her back. Understand?"

Klitzman was going to make sure that I jumped back into the world of the resort with both feet. I could always drop her off at the Punishment Tent, but I was sure that word of my circumvention of Klitzman's orders would get back to him. I looked at her attractive, beauteous form. Well, it was her or me.

The African guard had retrieved a brown robe for me and a pair of sandals. I slipped them on and then he handed me a slave leash and a gag. I stepped over to the unlucky female and attached the leash to her collar and then pulled her to her feet. I could see her body tremble in fear as she realized that she was the prizewinner that Klitzman had selected, although she dutifully kept her eyes closed and her mouth formed into the little 'o'. Her breasts swayed attractively as she rose. The shape of her mouth was conveniently conducive to reception of the thick, leather gag that I inserted and then buckled behind her head.

"Your cottage is all ready for you, Harry," Klitzman said as he munched the cunt smeared turkey meat in his mouth. "I want you down at transit at 8 A.M. sharp. Everything that you'll need will be there. The plane leaves at 8:30."

"So, where am I going?" I asked.

"On an adventure, Harry, that's where," Klitzman answered. He gave one of his patented belly laughs. I realized that was all I would get out of him for the time being and so I turned and made my exit, the unfortunate, big breasted, brown haired girl scurrying behind me.

With the soon to be very unhappy slave girl in tow, I made my way back to my cottage retracing the steps I had taken about three weeks before. It was late in the afternoon, maybe about 4. The air outside was as still as the breath from a statue and the humid air cloyed to my face and legs like cotton candy. I hadn't gone far before I had worked up a copious sweat.

3 to 5 p.m. was always the worst part of the day on our little island paradise. The sun wasn't at its hottest, but there was almost always an interregnum between the breeze running out from the mainland to the water and then back again at night as the cooler air over the South Atlantic rushed in to supplant the rising hot air over the land. Most of the guests and supervisors where indoors somewhere enjoying the air conditioning. It was also the time for shift change at many of the cafes and other entertainment facilities and bevies of bound beauties were making there way to and from the Slave Center. A few of them gave me a startled look as they passed clip clopping hurriedly on the brick pathways. "Oh, yes," I said to myself. "Harry's back." I must have looked like death warmed over.

I hoped that word would get back somehow to Carol of my resurrection. I had to somehow think of how to convey to her without making actual contact that I had received her loving messages and was grateful for them. I would have to work something out.

My mind quickly shifted to my recollection and sorrow for the loss of Mary. My mood grew darker and darker as I approached my cottage. How had I ever let myself get so emotionally involved with the fate of a slave girl, I asked myself. What a fool I had been to believe that I had carved out a little piece of paradise that the three of us, me, Mary and Carol could share. No one was safe on Klitzman's island. Even the guests, who relished the freedom to treat the abject slave girls any way that they pleased sans consequences for their acts, were irretrievably caught in Klitzman's web. What one of them could ever deny Klitzman or his minions anything once they had been here? For the real world would not share the insouciance with which the males who came to the island for fun and play witnessed and participated in the fiendish excesses which occurred here.

At one of the crossroads to the interminable pathways that crisscrossed the resort, I paused to let a little parade go by. There were five or six amused looking men all dressed in the blue robes of guests marching down the pathway. In their center was a tall, thin, naked, gagged and bound slave girl with long, black hair and small, little girl breasts being led with a leash by a seemingly gleeful man in the front. I could see the outline of her ribs through the pale skin that covered her slender frame. I knew where the men were headed.

The path they were on led to the Punishment Tent. I wasn't really a tent, but, rather, a small amphitheater covered by a large canopy where amused guests could sit and watch while pretty, young women were lashed and beaten. And it wasn't really for punishments, the punishments, those meant to convey to the recipient a dire warning of terrible consequences appurtenant to disobedience or slothful behavior were conducted by guards or supervisors elsewhere. It was for the pleasure of the guests, a place where they could bring a lovely and watch her suffer a vicious pummeling of her flesh at the hands of an expert. The men who were crossing the pathway in front of me, all middle aged, dark skinned Mediterranean types, had apparently decided to partake in the novelty of watching the black haired girl's writhing, anguished contortions as she was treated to a lesson with a lash. The girl's eyes were wide and troubled as she passed, knowing what her immediate future had in store for her. She exhibited, however, no physical reticence to accompany the merry band, a sin that would have doubled her upcoming travail and maybe brought her, in addition, a round with one of the supervisors or guards later underground.

I let the men and their victim pass and then continued on my way to my cottage. My stomach was growling with hunger, but I did not stop at any of the cafes on my way. I wanted to get out of the public portion of the resort as soon as possible. The thought of witnessing my little Carol being led by the real or invented, nasty Russian that Klitzman had described, or any other of the hard edged, amoral males of the resort to her next round of abuse would have been too much to take. I had a job to do, as despicable as it might be, and I was going to do it and then flood my belly with a half a quart of scotch.

The familiar shape of my cottage soon appeared before me. I led the brunette up the several steps to the small porch and then swung the door open. I had to stop for a moment, taken aback by the form of a small, shapely slave girl kneeling in my living room, her ankle fastened to a ring in the floor in the very spot where Carol and Mary had so often greeted me. She had long, brown hair that was gathered in a ponytail behind her head and, just for an instant, my heart leapt at the thought that Carol had been returned to me. On closer inspection, I saw that she was a stranger, not my Carol after all, but another unfortunate wench, her hands bound behind her, her mouth gagged, waiting expectantly and fearfully for my arrival.

Klitzman thought of everything. He was the great corruptor. I could resolve not to partake any further in the injustices and cruelties of the resort all I wanted. But he knew that my resolution would be like sand in an hourglass, destined to pour away almost as soon as it was made.

I ignored the frightened looking young girl as I dragged my prisoner to the center of the room. A chain appropriate for mounting a slave girl for beating hung down from the 10' high ceiling. I quickly unfastened the brunette's hands from behind her back and refastened then up in the air above her head. I pulled the chain taut so that she was standing on the tips of her bright red, high heel shoes. She gave out a little whine from behind her gag as I did so and I noticed that her eyes were still firmly shut from when we had been back at Klitzman's. No one had told her to open them and, being a dutiful slave fearful of adding to her unfortunate circumstances, she had kept them closed. That suited me fine. I had no desire to make eye contact with my victim. In fact, I wanted to blot out her humanity, forget that she was a feeling, thinking, human being. She was an object to be used as her masters saw fit, even to her demise.

A cabinet against the far wall contained the equipage of cruelty and I took out a soft, black, knitted hood from one of the drawers. Standing behind her, I drew the form fitting adornment over her head and tied it off below her neck with the drawstring in its base. Having rendered the trembling slave girl fully anonymous, I took a moment to admire her soft, curvaceous flesh and plentiful pulchritude.

As I said, her breasts were full and ripe, large by the island's standards, which seemed to favor a full but not overly generous display of femininity. Her mounds hung heavily from her torso, swaying gently as her body gave off tremors of fear. I took hold of their fullness, relishing the feel of their warmth and their spongy firmness in my coarse hands. She gave a little start when my flesh made contact with hers, as if certain that her torment was about to commence. But I was entranced by her beauteous form and I wanted to savor the tell tale tingling of arousal in my loins that had been sparked by her desirable form.

I massaged the large, heavy orbs gently and rubbed my thumbs across her stiffened nipples. They were fat and long and were surrounded by large, round ponds of dark, smooth skin. Her fear had raised little goose bumps around the circumference of her areolas, and their roughness contrasted with the silky feel of the skin surrounding her nipples. I guessed that the girl was maybe 24 or 25 from the relative freshness of her skin and the way that her taut, heavy breasts defied the pull of gravity. But faintly on her skin I could see the tell tale signs of her prior abuse, long, thin faint lines of paler flesh, a slight discoloration here and there. She had undoubtedly been through alot.

I quickly put thoughts of who she was and what she had gone through from my mind. That way was madness. I was about to scour her body with cruel implements of pain, to do my duty to my master and put myself back into his good graces. I ran my hands down her belly and over her round hips. Her brownish skin was soft and smooth. When I dropped a hand between her thighs, she obediently opened them even though the spreading of her legs forced more weight on her outstretched hands. Someone had decreed that she would wear a small trim of her mature hair around the entrance to her cleft and a small, short beard above it. I let my fingers linger in her tiny bush enjoying the feel of the silky growth. After a few moments, I let my hand slide down slowly until I had her fleshy mons cupped in my hand. It was warm and tender, firm and not yet plush with the signs of arousal. I sensed the woman relax her body and as I began to stroke the fuzzy lips that guarded the entrance to her womb, her pussy began to obediently moisten.

She was a well trained slut. In the midst of her fear she had taken her mind to that place that would allow her juices to flow, ease my penetration. Within a few moments I was able to urge her fat love lips aside and slide my fingers along the length of her slick gash and then plunge within her.

The girl's breathing had become heavy from the combination of the effects of my ministrations to her twat and her apprehension of what she knew was to come. The cloth that covered her face fluttered with each labored breath and her breasts began to dance before my eyes. I wanted to see her ass and so I took my free hand and forced her to twirl in place so that her back was to me. Her rear globes were firm and soft. I caressed them gently, or as gently as my hard, calloused hands would allow. I rubbed my fingers over the two inch high indentation on her upper right buttock, the site of her marking as a being that dwelled in her own flesh only at the sufferance of her masters. The cursive "*k*" that had been burned there, and, like on all of the other female initiates to our club, had been smeared with red dyed ointment immediately after the wound had been inflicted. The angry, red, rococo letter stood out from her flesh like a beacon to my lusts. My cock was growing harder by the second as a result of my examination of her flesh. My passions were rising. It seemed a good time to begin our little dance.

I stepped back and drew the reddish brown robe from my body and tossed it aside. The other slave girl, who had been watching me wide eyed, trembling on her own behalf, gave a little jump at my sudden movement. I looked at her and guessed that Klitzman, or Anthony or Rukimo, or whoever had selected this particular piece of naked, female property for my use, had sent me another rookie, a girl who was new to her bindings, probably her first time above ground since she had been sent to the Slave Center for indoctrination as to her new duties after suffering her initial training in Rukimo's domain. She had been undoubtedly told the consequences of disappointing one of the demanding masters she would serve here. Well, that was no business of mine either. Her sensibilities were not of my concern.

I stepped out of my sandals and strode back over to the cabinet against the far wall. Opening the doors to the shelves on the top, I took stock of the array of instruments of pain within it. I had not used them much when Mary and Carol had been my guests. Occasionally I had brought home and whipped one of the other slave girls from the resort, one of the serving girls from my club or a waitress from one of the cafes, or even a pretty young thing that I had espied on her way to here or there. But I had usually done no more than warm up their flesh in order to stoke my lusts. Today, I would be doing much more.

The sun had begun to set around my cottage and the light had begun to fade, creating a somber, eerie atmosphere inside. Klitzman had instructed me that he wanted the girl striped with evidence of the lash and black and blue when she was returned and so that meant that I would need to select one of the long, thin whips from the closet as well as a leather encased rising crop. But with which one to start?

I decided that I would begin with the whip. I took out a 3' long thin, leather encase reed that tapered to a small point on the end. The thinness of the weapon would assure long, narrow lacerations on her body. I swished it through the air to test it and both women gave out little whimpers of apprehension as it whirred through the air. The slave girl kneeling on the floor had tears forming in her eyes as I'm sure she was recalling her days in training and hoped desperately that the switch was not meant for her. I gave the whip another test swing and it made a sharp, hissing sound as it passed through the air in my otherwise silent cottage. I was ready.

The dangling female's body tremors had increased in intensity as she tried to steel herself for what was to come. I circled her body slowly, using my free hand to caress her bulbous breasts, her hips and her fine, round rump, relishing the soft feel of her tender skin. I turned suddenly on my heel and gave the unfortunate woman a fierce blow from the whip across the front of her graceful, well formed thighs. The marriage of the leather to her flesh made a loud 'crack!' as the whip struck her, followed immediately by a loud wail of pain only partially obscured by the gag that filled her mouth. Her body stiffened and then she began to dance on her toes, using her frenetic physical actions to try and somehow endure the painful sensation of her torn skin. The whip left a long, narrow strip of bright red along the front of her coffee colored thighs.

While the whimpering girl tried to regain some equanimity regarding her predicament, I continued to circle around her. I ran my hand over her taut, firm belly, over her hip and then her back. When I returned to the front, I let the whip fly once more, this time across her firm, full breasts. "Crack!" The sound of the whip kissing flesh resounded through the small room. The girl gave out a deep, long, forlorn wail as the sudden pain coursed through her. Her hands writhed in her confinements above her and her black, hooded head turned side to side in her agony. A long line of abused flesh arose on her breasts, just over her nipples. Her legs were shaking and she tried to press them together to still her body's quakes. I struck her again as I turned the corner on her left side, this time laying the lash across her plump, pleasing rear globes. And then again on the front of her thighs and then, as I circled behind her once more, across the small of her back.

The poor woman's voice was now in a continuous howl which lowered slightly as I took the time to decide where to lay the next blow and then raised again as the cruel leather weapon tore into her. Her body was sweating heavily and her torso had developed a sheen of perspiration, making her breasts, belly and back shine in the fading light. My temperature was rising higher and higher with each fierce laceration of her flesh. God help me, but the sight of a beautiful woman in the throes of agony at my hands drove my lusts. I continued to batter her defenseless body, my cock standing rigid as a soldier on parade. Each fierce, agony producing stroke of the whip seemed to fuel my eagerness to add another to the girl's torment.

I had given the pitiable, desirable female more than twenty five lashings before my brain resumed control of my passions. She was uttering low, mournful, muffled pleas in whatever was her native language. Her body looked like someone had tried to scratch it out with red ink. Her breasts were red lined over, above and under her rigid, fat nipples. Her belly was thatched with angry red lines as were her thighs, back and rear. Here and there, small trails of blood dribbled from her wounds. I took a long, deep breath. Enough, I thought.

The young slave girl who had been kneeling on the floor when I arrived was crying uncontrollably. What level of Hell have I been delivered to, she was probably thinking. Her kneeling body came to rigid attention when she saw that she had drawn my gaze. I was sure that if she could have made her pretty body disappear right in front of me she would have.

Ignoring her, I stepped over to the breakfront that sat along one wall and removed a bottle of scotch from the cabinet. My heart was pumping wildly and my chest was heaving from a combination of my passions and my exertions. I poured out a generous portion of the golden hued liquid into a glass and I downed it all in one gulp. I was damned and I knew it. What god could forgive me for what I had done? Was my continued existence really so important after all? I was under the devil's thumb and doing his work, all in the specious conceit that I was acting to assuage the predicament of another slave girl who, in all probability, would someday meet an undesirable, unhappy fate, just like Mary.

The hot scotch burned as it went down. My mind welcomed the numbing effects of the alcohol as it raced into my bloodstream. I felt a surge of reinforcement of my original, self deceptive, hypocritical prevarications. Whatever I did to this forlorn slave girl who was dangling from her wrists, moaning and weeping in my little cottage, mattered naught. If it wasn't me tormenting her earthly existence, it would be someone else. If it wasn't today that she underwent a cruel, heinous abuse of her flesh, it would be tomorrow. I poured myself another three inches of the devil's brew and downed it in one gulp. I looked at the swaying, battered body of the female as the liquor soothed my qualms. She was swaying slightly, her red high heeled shoes standing on their tippy toes. Black and blue.

Klitzman wanted her black and blue. I would kowtow to his demonic will.

All of a sudden, the pitiful female became a surrogate for the fat man's flesh. She became the embodiment of all that I hated about Klitzman, the evil I saw around me and, most of all, myself. I put down my glass and, tossing the whip aside, went back to the cabinet that held the other implements of pain and degradation that came as standard amenities to my little home. I picked out a heavy, leather encase riding crop. It was a good two inches around. I did away with the preliminaries and went immediately to work.

The abject female gave out a loud agonized groan as I delivered a crushing blow to her body across her heavy breasts. They flattened as the riding crop descended on them, vibrating wildly as they resumed their shape. I struck her across the front of her thighs, on her belly, on her sides, the instrument colliding with her ribs. I delivered blows across her back, the back of her legs and shins and even on the muscles of her arms. Her moans of anguish emerged from her tight gag and filled the room. It was long and continuous, growing louder each time the cruel rod struck home and then whimpering off to an unhappy murmur. She would be black and blue all right. Her body would be the emblem of my damnation, a symbol of what I had become.

After about ten blows I stopped. My chest was heaving and my mind was feverish. My cock was aching with need. I tossed the riding crop aside and stepped over to the sobbing, young slave girl who cowered helplessly in the corner of the room. "Get up!" I yelled at her. Timorously, her body quaking, her eyes recording her terror, the girl struggled to her feet. I knelt and released her ankle chain. "Get in the bedroom," I commanded churlishly.

The girl, panicked, turned and ran into the next room, happy to be out of my presence if only for an instant. The brown haired woman who I had been tormenting hung almost lifelessly in her chains. Her hooded, black covered head hung down, her chin riding on her chest. The places where I had struck her were colored a deep maroon. Her blood would pool there and die. Within the hour, deep purple wounds would be displayed. I had done my job. Klitzman would be pleased not only at the torment that the girl had suffered, but also at the confirmation of my status as his corrupted, perverse minion.

I strode resolutely into the bedroom. The girl was standing at the foot of the bed, too frightened to do anything more than perform the literal act that I had commanded. I took hold of her shoulders and spun her body so that her back was to me and released the confinements that held her hands prisoners behind her back. Taking hold of the ring in her collar, I dragged her to the bed and flung her onto it. Her body tumbled as she struck the mattress and she gave out a frightened squeal behind her gag. I quickly leapt after her and, taking her by her long, brown ponytail, pulled her to her knees. She gave out a muffled cry from the pain of her strained hair. I tilted her head back and took a good look at her. Her eyes were widened with her fear. Her conical, coffee cup sized breasts were taut as twin drums and her tiny nipples were as rigid as little stones. Her arms were raised at her sides, her slender, diminutive hands clasped into miniature fists, useless in preventing my abuse of her.

Reaching my other hand behind the girl's head, I loosened the gag that had till now covered the lower portion of her face and filled her mouth with a long, thick wad of leather. I tossed the implement aside and took in her frightened, miserating face. She had thin, pale lips that

were trembling. Her face was wet with the flow of tears. I
grabbed her delicate cheeks with my large, hardened hand
and crushed them with a death like grip. Leaning over, I
thrust my tongue onto her mouth, pressing my fevered lips
upon hers. She moaned and her body squirmed as I
explored her hot, moist interior, invading the space that
had recently been filled by the harsh gag. Her tongue
obediently tried to keep pace with mine, but I forced it
aside with my own, scouring her mouth's interior, drawing
my lust higher and higher.

Overcome with my need, I pushed the girl down onto
her back on the bed. The bedclothes had been thoughtfully
turned down by someone and she lay atop the smooth, cool
sheets as I grasped her hands and fastened them to the
chain that led from the headboard. Her hands writhed
helplessly above her as I took my right hand and stroked it
along the length of her desirable, proffered flesh. I took
hold of each of her firm, enticing orbs in turn, squeezing
them tightly until she moaned in pain. I drifted my hand
across her taut, flat belly which fluttered nervously as I
touched it, anticipating my impending possession of her
loins.

The girl was curvaceous yet slender, pale of skin, her
thighs taut and lean. She spread them obediently as I
delved my hand between them, taking hold of her naked,
hairless lower lips between my fingers and giving them a
hearty squeeze. She gave out an anguished squeal and her
hips rose from the pain. I watched her face, her fear and
pain etched into it, her delicate features contorted and
almost grotesque. Relenting my grip, I began to probe
between the now injured love lips and pushed my fingers
into her crevasse. It was dry and tight, but I continued to
stroke and fondle her quim, interposing my digits deeper
and deeper into her hot tunnel until her moisture began to

flow. Her eyes were clamped shut and I could see that she had taken herself where obedient, compliant little slave girls go when performing their duty of preparing their cunts for abuse.

After a minute or so, I could see that the girl's passions had begun to grow. Her hips began to thrust back at my relentless, pussy filling fingers, her back was arching and her face had become flush. She had been trained well to perform for her masters and I saw that she was suitable for my penetration of her with my hardened, fuck ready prick.

I climbed my body atop the girl's and spread her pale, quivering thighs wider with my knees. Taking my joint in my right hand, I guided it to her now moist and loose gash and rudely thrust myself inside her. Her body rose and trembled as I slid deep into her quim. Her eyes had opened and her quivering lips had parted. She stared back at me, her unhappiness at her abuse written on her face, a face that could not hide her arousal. Taking hold of her cheeks with my hand, I regained possession of her mouth, slithering my thick, writhing tongue inside it as I began to drive my cock piston-like along the walls of her hot, pleasure giving sex.

My thrusts at the girl's pussy were relentless and hard. My body seemed ready to explode with the built up emotions of the last two weeks, the loss of my beloved playmates, the despair of my imprisonment, doom always seemingly moments away, my self hatred at so readily succumbing to Klitzman's demonic yoke and the lusts and passions that had arose in me as a result of my heinous abuse of the other woman's flesh. I roared as my cock began to throb and pulse within her. She was coming too, and her thighs and legs thrashed wildly on the bed, pressing against the sides of my legs, squeezing me with all the feeble force she was capable of, grinding her heels in my back. While moaning her involuntary pleasure into my mouth, her torso writhed and squirmed underneath me as I poured what seemed to be a never ending stream of my hot spunk deep into her womb.

When my ejaculations ebbed, a wave of relief and torpor flowed through my body. The weeks of tension and fear had fled me. I felt like a wrung out cloth, my muscles and my mind emptied of all will. As my cock softened within the still moaning girl's crevasse, I fell asleep.

CHAPTER FIVE

The body of the slave girl was still beneath me when I awoke. I was groggy at first, not sure of where I was. Her soft flesh was mashed beneath my body and I could feel and hear her troubled breath as a result of bearing my not inconsiderable weight upon her throughout the night. Dawn had apparently broken a short while ago and I looked over at the clock near my bed and saw that it was a little after 6 A.M.

I had fully intended to clean myself up and get a decent meal when I had returned to my cottage the day before, but the stress of my long imprisonment and several ounces of premier, single malt scotch, not to mention an explosive orgasm, had made slumber overcome me. Today I was going on a trip to who knows where and I realized that I would have to get up right away if I was going to meet the 8:00 appointment that Klitzman had set for me.

I rolled off the supine girl much to her relief. I'm sure that it was a good news, bad new sort of thing, good that my heavy body was off of her so that she wouldn't suffocate and bad because I was awake and perhaps intent on imposing more abuse on her. Although my cock was hard, cleanliness was my top priority. I felt like something the cat had dragged in. My mouth was dry and raunchy and I could smell my own foul odors. It must have been hell for the girl to inhale my scents throughout the night, too scared to even wriggle out from under my comparably massive frame.

She was watching me with a good deal of interest as I rose off of the bed. My bladder was full to burst and I was sure that hers was too. I felt a bit of compunction over my treatment of her the night before and so I released her hands and told her to go use the slave bathroom and freshen herself up a bit.

When I came out of my bathroom she was kneeling dutifully in the hallway, her hands spread palm up on her thighs, her knees apart. She had washed the remnants of her tears from her face and managed to brush her hair. She still looked pitiful as she stared up at me apprehensively. Two weeks ago I might have said some kind words to her to alleviate her distress, but something in me had changed. Looking at her, I couldn't care less how she felt. She had her troubles and I had mine.

I retrieved her gag from the bedroom and inserted it roughly between her dainty lips, belting it tightly behind her head. I motioned for her to lie on the floor and I fastened her wrists behind her and then locked her ankles together. She could lie there and await my pleasure.

The feel of the hot shower was delightful. I let the water run over my body for about five minutes before I did anything to wash myself. I could have had the slave girl attend to me, but I really didn't want to have anyone else around to disturb my silent enjoyment of one of the great blessings of civilization. When I began to feel human again, I lathered up my body thoroughly. I rinsed and washed my longer than I liked it hair and then brushed my teeth. You don't know how wonderful it is to be able to brush your teeth until you have been deprived of that opportunity for twenty-one days or so. My gums were sore when I was finished, but I felt for the first time in a while that my mouth was not a trash bin. I gargled thoroughly and then brushed my hair. I then took my time shaving, enjoying the hot water and soap upon my face and the distinctive feel of the sharp blade as it cleaned away my three weeks' growth and left behind a clean, smooth face.

When done, I took a good look in the mirror. My eyes were still dark and foreboding, not that they had ever been bright and cheerful. I saw a few new wrinkles. The scar on my right cheek seemed somehow more pronounced. I had certainly lost weight and my face had a certain gaunt look to it. I knew that I would fill out again quickly, but my experiences had certainly been recorded in my mien. I looked a little harder, more capable of evil, than I had before. I was never a guy who you would slide over to and start a chat with if you saw me sitting at a bar. But now, if you saw me there, you might just turn around and leave.

My belly was rumbling with the need for sustenance. I knew that I could get a full meal at one of the early morning cafes down at the resort and so I made ready to leave my cottage. I didn't know where my little journey would take me. The last time Klitzman sent me somewhere I almost met my maker, something that would have been extremely prejudicial to my eternal interests. I mean, my copybook was severely blotted and there were virtually no entries on the good deed side of the ledger. I wasn't sure whether there was an afterlife or not, but I liked it here and didn't want to find out for sure just yet.

I left the bathroom and, stepping over the prone, bound body of the naked slave girl, retrieved a clean brown robe from my bedroom. I passed her again on the way out. Her helplessness was enticing. I considered for the moment taking advantage of her supple, beauteous flesh before I made my way down to the resort but thought better of it. I didn't want to be late for my appointment and also didn't want to rush what would be my first relaxed, sumptuous meal in a long time. She looked up at me forlornly from the floor. I could have taken the time to make her more comfortable while she waited for someone to come and get her and return her to the Slave Center, but why? I was doing her a favor really. I was not the worst master she would serve during her useful life at the resort, nor the cruelest. The sooner she became acclimated to just what she had become, the better.

Went I came into the living room to retrieve my sandals, I saw the dangling and hooded body of my victim from the night before. Her black hooded head twitched in response to my approach. Her body was a roadmap of abuse, large pools and oceans of black and blue marks over her breasts, belly and thighs, all connected by long, thin thoroughfares of angry, red lines. I was sure that Klitzman would not be disappointed at my artistry.

The girl had been standing all night on her tippy toes and I was sure that she was in a world of discomfort and pain. It would be a difficult, long walk back to Klitzman's for her. I released her hands from her bindings over her head and her whole body sagged as she let her weight back down onto her feet. She stumbled and placed one of her hands on my shoulder for balance, pulling it back immediately as if in horror of her own presumptuousness. Touching a master without permission was a whipping offense. But I was not in the mood to add to the young woman's misfortunes.

Reconnecting her wrists behind her back while she regained her balance, I then attached the leash I had used the day before to her collar. I removed the black hood that had covered her face. She looked at me with sorrow and foreboding at what the new day would bring for her. She had to blink her eyes several times to acclimate her vision to renewed light. I noticed for the first time that she had blue, sparkling eyes, eyes that once undoubtedly gleamed with happiness and pleasure. I felt a wave of remorse flow through me for what I had done to her and for what she was condemned to. But I withheld any gestures of compassion. What good would that have done?

When I turned to leave the cottage, I saw that the other slave girl had her head craned up and was watching me, probably to make sure I was really leaving. Curiosity in a slave girl was grossly inappropriate. I released the leash of the girl I had beaten and walked down the hall. I could see from the prone slave girl's large, brown eyes that she was unhappy that she had drawn my attention. I knelt down and pulled the hood that the other slave had been wearing over her head and drew it tight around her neck. She would await the next development in her slave life in darkness, free to contemplate the lesson in brutality she had witnessed the night before and my callous use of her. I took hold of her ankles, dragging her into the living area. I could hear her whining as her pretty, little breasts were scraped across the rug. When she was under the chain that had held the wrists of the other slave girl throughout the night, I dropped her while I adjusted the chain so I could attach her ankles to it. Once fastened, I pulled the chain high again until her black, hooded head was free of the floor.

Her upside down, naked, beauteous form was swaying slightly, her bound arms writhing behind her back, her delicate, chestnut colored hair flowing out from the edges of the black hood. I didn't know how long it would be until one of the native stewards would come by to get her, but, in the meantime, she would be free to assay her fate and rue her misfortune. Next time she would mind her own business.

I led the brunette I had whipped out the front door of the cottage and waited patiently as she struggled to descend the three short steps to the pathway. I realized that she probably had to relieve herself and so before taking her on her way let her step over to the grass. I snapped my fingers and pointed downwards. Obediently, the girl slowly lowered herself into a crouch, her knees spread wide, moaning as she stretched the abused muscles of her thighs and shins. In a moment, I could hear the sound of a strong, forceful splash onto the bright green grass as she emptied herself. I looked down and saw the bright yellow stream emitting from her urethra. Even slave girls had needs, and it would be a poor and, eventually, unhappy master who did not see to them. The girls were only human, if barely, after all, and without proper attention, they would soon be shitting and pissing all over the place.

The girl let her head lean back as she peed. Her eyes were closed to half slits as she experienced obvious relief. Her bruised and battered body made her look like some exotic, piebald creature. When the last drops came dribbling from her loins, I grabbed a large leaf from a small tree that sat in the yard in front of my cottage and used it to wipe her clean. I tossed the leaf aside and pulled her back to a standing position. Then, tugging on the leash, I began to lead her back to her hellish home.

The guards outside of Klitzman's domain seemed impressed with the brutal artwork that adorned the young woman's body. I handed over the leash to one of them and the tall, black, muscular African took a moment to admire the bruises and lacerations that covered her. He exchanged some banter with his confrere in their native patois and laughed. I had hoped that the girl would at least get to rest and recuperate before her next round of abuse, but I could see that that was doubtful. As they guided her into the little hut that stood next to the gate, I put her fate out of my mind and walked away.

I was sitting at one of the outdoor cafes and eating a large order of flapjacks and bacon when Anthony came upon me. I had had many dealings with the suave, senior supervisor. He had been my guide to the fine points of the resort when I first arrived. He was dark of complexion, short, curly, dark, black hair, a refined, handsome face. He wore, like I did, the brown robe of a supervisor and he sat down next to me without ceremony. When the blond haired slave waitress came over, he ordered a cup of coffee. When she left on her errand, he spoke to me.

"You're one lucky motherfucker, Harry," he said to me. "Not many get to see the inside of Klitzman's dungeon and live to talk about it."

I had a mouthful of pancakes and mumbled an agreement with his observation. The naked girl came back with his coffee and I detected a reticence in her demeanor as if merely being in the senior supervisor's presence would infect her with bad karma. She was a sweet looking thing with long, straw blond hair and a little tuft of pubic growth over her plump love lips. Her high heels made her long, svelte legs seem longer. She retreated to the waitress station as soon as she could.

"If I were you, Harry," Anthony continued, "I wouldn't fuck up this mission. You're on pretty thin ice as it is."

I had downed the mouthful of pleasantly tasting sustenance drenched with sweet maple syrup. I could feel the pounds that I had lost coming back as I sat there. I picked up a strip of the thick, crisp bacon and took a bite. Heaven.

"I'll do my best," I answered. "But it's hard to gauge my chances when I don't know what the fuck I'm going to be doing. The last time you guys almost got me killed."

"It's because of your successful evasion of your untimely demise and the other men with you that you've been given a second chance, Harry," Anthony returned. "You'll be fully briefed by Ms. Bordolinski once you get in the air. This way if someone interferes with the operation at the other end we'll know that it's not because you told anyone here. Loose lips sink ships, Harry. But I will tell you this. Watch out for little Ms. Natanya. She's one of Mr. K's favorites but she's got a mind of her own and, in my estimation, is capable of anything. You're to bring home the goods, Harry, and if you don't, don't come back. Find some little corner of the world and live life to the fullest, because we'll catch up to you sooner or later. And it won't be pretty."

A chill went down my spine. I was living in a nest of tarantulas and I was going on a trip with a black widow spider to God knows where to do God knows what. There were still two flapjacks on my plate and a couple of strips of bacon. I had thought about leaving my breakfast fare unfinished in consideration of my girlish figure, but I realized that the number of pancakes that I might have the opportunity to eat between now and the end of all things could be severely finite. I decided to finish them.

My stomach had a decided bulge as Anthony led me over to the Transit Hut, as they called it. It was on the edge of the resort near the main gate, a gate that I had entered many months ago innocent of all that pertained within. The Transit Hut was where outgoing slave girls were packaged for their trips to their new homes and guys like me were issued real clothes so that we could reenter the world. When we stepped into the small structure, two naked slave girls were lying on the floor hogtied and hooded. One of the staff was preparing travel crates for them.

"Ah, Mr. Harry," a thin, white clad, black man called out. The staff occupied a sort of limbo in the resort. They dressed in all white: white sneakers, white slacks and white t-shirts. They preformed many of the service tasks around the resort, delivering slave girls here and there, supervising the kitchens, making sure that the bars were stocked, that sort of thing. They did not strictly have the right to use the girls while in the resort, but none of the girls would have, I was sure, the temerity to complain if she was given a taste of their hard, black meat when none of the guests or supervisors were around. The staff had their own recreational facility on the other side of the gate staffed by girls who had lost their bloom. And I was also sure that none of the girls would want to risk ending up there after she had displeased one of them.

"Over here, Mr. Harry," the slender, African advised me. His English was perfect except for a slight lilt to his speech. He had a finely trimmed beard that ran along the edge of his chin.

On the counter where the man directed me was a large, canvas travel bag. Next to it were arrayed several piles of clothing and a travel kit. There was soap, toothpaste and a toothbrush, a pile of bright, white, jockey underwear, a few collared polo shirts of various pastel shades, two pair of tan, cotton slacks, a hair brush, a razor and shaving cream, etc., etc.

"I just wanted you to see what you've got before I packed it all up," the black skinned man told me. "You can put on some clothes now and I'll pack the rest. You'll get some more clothes appropriate for your destination when you get there," he added.

Pastel polo shirts were really not my line. But who was I to bitch? I was lucky just to be alive. They could have dressed me in a clown's outfit right down to 18" long funny shoes if they wanted.

After I dressed, choosing a very light green shirt and donning the brown, hand tooled Italian shoes that were given me, Anthony directed me to a private room. There was a long, oaken table with some chairs around it. On the table was a thin, black, leather briefcase, a silver .45 caliber semi-automatic sitting in a brown, leather shoulder holster, a box of bullets, a spare clip and a neatly banded stack of $100.00 bills. This, I guessed, had something to do with my mission.

Anthony stepped up to the table and, turning the combination to the briefcase, opened it. Lying in neat little rows, encased in clear, round, plastic cases, were more Kügerrands than I had ever seen in my life. "Oh, oh," I thought. Apparently I was to be responsible for a small fortune in gold. I would be the target of every hot headed stick up artist in the world. I would need the .45, and more.

"Take a good look, Harry," Anthony told me. "Take some out and get a good look at them."

I reached in and picked up one of the rolls. I flipped open the case and took out one of the one ounce gold pieces and weighed it in my hand. The shiny coin, mounted with the profile of some 19th century, bearded fellow, Mr. Krüger, I presumed, neatly serrated around its edges, had the feel of wealth and power. Gold was the stuff that dreams were made of, isn't that what they said? Since the dawn of history, man had lusted after its glittery enticement. There was a feeling of portent in the room, a moment of silence in respect for the metal's great power and allure. No matter what the situation, no matter if civilization itself came tumbling down, gold would be always, well, worth its weight.

"Cool, huh," Anthony said. Cool indeed. A man could buy a lot of disappearance with this much gold. Why was God always putting temptation in my way? Didn't he know how weak I was? Didn't Klitzman?

"The gold is to be delivered to a certain friend of ours in exchange for a certain something. That's all you need to know now. I don't have to tell you to guard it with your life, Harry, because I know that you already know that. And remember, it may be the universal currency, but someone dumping 800 Kügerrands or even spreading them around thinly will sooner or later be found. You get my drift?"

I heard Anthony speaking but I didn't really hear him. I was still mesmerized by the sparkling array of coins on the table in front of me. 800 Kügerrands at about 400 bucks each meant about $320,000. I'm sure it was chicken feed to Klitzman, but it was a fortune to me. And big, fat, greedy gluttons like Klitzman were often notorious misers. He would agonize over their loss like Emperor Augustus over his lost eagles.

"Yeah," I finally answered.

"There's $5,000 in cash for expenses. You don't have to spend it all because it's all there. But if you get in a jam, it could provide the juice to see you out of it. Mr. K is counting on you, Harry. Don't fuck up."

Anthony retrieved the roll of Krügers from my hand and returned them to the valise. He took 5 hundred dollar bills from the stack and placed the rest inside the case. "Put this in your pocket, Harry. Use it for incidentals," he said.

I took the neat, crisp bills from his hand and folded them and put them in my pocket. I looked at the heavy armament on the table. "I think I'll be a little conspicuous, wherever I'm going, with that strapped on me," I said. "Don't you have anything smaller?"

"You'll need the throw weight, Harry. Just the sound of this thing going off will make a lot of guys run for the hills. You'll have a sports jacket to wear to cover it up."

"Well, I'd feel a whole lot better if I had something for close in work," I told him. "Maybe a Beretta, the one I used a few weeks ago."

"We'd prefer it if you used your wits to get yourself out of any trouble, Harry. One pistola is enough."

"Well, how about a shiv?" I asked hopefully. "Something that'll do the job quietly. I mean a .45 will wake up the whole neighborhood."

"Okay, Harry, I'll see what we have."

Anthony left me in the room to stare at the now closed case of gold for a few minutes. He came back with the bearded African staff member from the outer room. He was carrying a tray that held a half dozen shiny, new switchblades. I never really dabbled in knife work when I worked for Tony in Atlantic City, but when I was growing up being able to handle a finely honed blade was *di rigueur*. And in the joint it was all the protection you could get.

I sampled the array of stabulatory devices and after opening and closing them, getting an appreciation of their balance and heft, I picked out a ruby red handled switch with a 7" long blade. I popped it open and closed it a few times. "This'll do," I concluded.

"Great!" Anthony applauded and clapped me on the shoulder. "Now do a good job and everyone will be in love with you again when you get back. Okay, Harry?"

"Okay," I mumbled, slipping the knife in my pants pocket. It weighed a little heavily but I would get used to it.

We went back into the outer room. There was a very sharply tailored, tan sports jacket there waiting for me. Anthony had brought out the hardware and I strapped the holster around my shoulders and then put on the jacket. He had put the extra clip and the box of bullets in the valise with the gold and the cash. The jacket had been specially tailored to take into account the bulge of a weapon and when I looked in the mirror I could hardly notice it. But anyone with any real experience would still spot it right away. I guess that was the intent. The .45 was my nuclear bomb, the point was not to have to use it.

The final touch was a silver banded, black Bulgari watch with bright, white numerals and a lot of fancy dials and shit that I would never know how to use. After many months, I was now accoutered in the fineries of civilization once again.

Anthony drove me through the gates of hell that regulated entrance into the resort and down along the coastal road that led to the island's airport. I took the time to acquaint myself with my new identity. Anthony had handed me a wallet containing a passport, driver's license, some fake credit cards and even a library card for some guy named Harry Lime. I was pleased to be able to retain my first name moniker, but was unhappy about being named after a fruit. Anthony assured me it was a name with an appropriate provenance.

We pulled up to the tarmac in the little SUV that Anthony piloted and I stepped out, taking the fifty pound briefcase and he canvas bag holding all of my belongings in the world. He gave me a nod of good luck and sped wordlessly away. The jet was running its engines, warming up for take off, and I climbed the ladder quickly, if cautiously, not wanting to end up sucked inside one of the large turbines. It was one of Klitzman's fleet of small private jets, used and useful in bringing guests and contraband to the island. I was greeted at the door by a tall, brunette "stewardess" who wore nothing but her collar and wrist and ankle bracelets and a little hat denoting her status. Coffee, tea or me was about to take on a whole new meaning. I let her show me one of the overhead compartments and I tossed my canvass bag inside it. The valise I decided would stay by my side.

There were about fifteen seats in the small jet, all set towards the back of the passenger compartment. Each seat had its own little table and swiveled around so that after take off the passengers could join into little social groups. I was the only passenger so far and, after removing my jacket and sliding the holster off of my shoulder, I took a seat near the front where I could get a good view of the in flight movie, assuming that there was one. I had settled in my chair and was sipping a hot cup of coffee from a paper cup that the stewardess had brought me when my travel companions boarded. Ms. Bordolinski was dressed identical to her costume of the day before. The girl, Celine, was dressed in a little, white, short sleeved dress with pink ribbons running along its hem and the cut out over her chest. Her hair was braided and curled up onto her head and she had small, pink berets on either side. I could tell from the girl's face that she was well beyond her prepubescent teens, but her attire gave her the look of a thirteen year old on her way to a birthday party. The skirt to the dress was short and reached a few inches above her knees. She wore sheer, white stockings that were thin enough so that the pinkish hue of the flesh beneath could be just seen. On her feet was a pair of low heeled, pink pumps. Yesterday, her hands had been free although they rested obediently in her lap during the time of my interview with Klitzman. Today, she wore shiny steel bracelets over her wrists that were connected by a sparkling steel chain about a foot or so long. It seemed incongruous in light of her otherwise adolescent attire. Its presence was decorative nonetheless. I rose to greet them.

"Mr. Harry," the black widow spat out. "I must say, you clean up well. I'm very pleased." I nodded a response.

"Celine, give Mr. Harry one of your prettiest curtsies," she told the innocent looking girl. The girl, without looking at her mistress, gave a small bending of her knees and gripped the front of the skirt to her dress with her bound hands and raised it slightly. There was a placid acceptance in her pretty, girlish face tinged with a note of fear. As she moved, I could see the feint hint of her bosom shift gently. She may have looked like a little girl, but there was an adequate pulchritude hidden behind her little girl attire. I wondered if I would get to see it.

At that moment the stewardess announced obsequiously that the plane was about to take off and asked whether we would please take our seats. The two women took seats next to mine and the plane's engine's rose in tone and the jet began to move. The older woman had ordered a cup of tea for herself and a cup of water for the girl and the waitress brought them and then retreated to the back of the plane to take her own seat. The jet soon reached the runway and, with a screech of tires and a roar of the engines, started its race for the sky.

As the plane climbed for altitude, I looked out of the window. Klitzman's island was quickly diminishing below us. I could see the huts and the mansions as they shrank in size. There was no evidence from this altitude of the dreadful nature of what happened there, just a pleasant resort set amidst the sparkling, surrounding South Atlantic. Far off in the distance I could see another jet circling in preparation for its landing, bringing more gay partiers for their holiday or, perhaps, more frightened, pretty, young women to serve as their playthings. Or both.

I remained silent sipping my coffee as we crossed over the narrow gap of water that separated the island from the mainland. Soon we were high above the jungle's canopy, a line of rough, green mountains looming some fifty or so miles ahead of us. I was back in the world. Sometime in the next few hours I would be discharged from the jet into the world of regular people, where young, beautiful girls could say no. It would take some getting used to.

About half an hour into our flight, the woman, Natanya, decided we should have a little chat. She spoke to the girl who was sitting between us. "Dear Celine," she said in a kindly, but authoritarian tone, "I'd like to speak to Mr. Harry in private. Why don't you go kneel in the corner over there for a little while like a good little girl?"

The girl looked up at her with discomfort. But she exhibited no rebellion at her mistress's command. She rose daintily and took a few quick steps over to the front of the passenger compartment and sank to her knees, her nose virtually rubbing into the corner.

"No," Natanya instructed her, "kneel with your forehead to the floor like I've shown you."

Celine shuffled back towards us on her knees and then leaned over obediently. Her delicate derriere strained the fabric of the back of her dress. I could see the soles of her shoes.

The stewardess had been kneeling the whole time in front of us, her hands on her knees, her thighs spread. I had been admiring her shapely tits and her naked, hairless quim for some time and trying to decide whether I should take advantage of the opportunity for some relief before we reached our destination. Who knew when the next time I would get some pussy? Going from several cum shots a day to zero was going to take some adjusting. But the idea of doing her in front of the spider woman kind of put me off.

Natanya spoke to her as well. "Go kneel in the other corner, slut," she ordered. Her voice had lost all of its sugar. The slave girl jumped to her feet and hurried over to the corner opposite Celine. She bent over and placed her forehead to the floor. She spread her knees so that her tender love lips were clearly visible between her outstretched thighs. My little boy gave a twitch at the vision of her two available apertures.

"Quite a pretty view, eh, Harry?" Natanya asked me, a hint of mockery in her voice. I guessed that she had read my reticence at taking advantage of the girl's warm, wet holes. I responded as noncommittally as I could.

"Quite nice, Ms. Bordolinski," I answered.

"Call me Natanya, Harry," the woman told me politely. "We're going to be together for a while and so we should be friends."

I remembered Anthony's warning about the beautiful, fulsome woman. I didn't want to get too friendly with her in case I had to kill her. Killing people you like can get old really fast. But I put on an air of amiability.

"My pleasure, Natanya," I answered her.

The woman rose from her seat and occupied the one next to me which her servant or slave or whatever she was had just vacated. The woman patted my hand like we were old pals. She gave me a cold blooded smile as she did so. "Do you like Celine, Harry? Isn't she pretty?"

"Quite pretty," I answered.

"Of course you haven't really had an opportunity yet to see all of her charms, have you, Harry?" the woman continued. She turned to the kneeling, supine girl. "Celine, Mr. Harry wants to get a look at your pretty, little bum. Lift up the back of your dress so that he can have a look."

The girl, whose hands were still bound in front of her with the decorative chain and bracelets, obediently turned her torso to the right so that she get a hold of the hem of her dress. Not without some effort, she wordlessly tugged it up until it was over her hip. She then leaned the other way and grabbed the dress at the other side and pulled it to her waist. She then dutifully resumed her position.

Revealed was a fine, pale expanse of taut, tender, pantyless flesh. Her globes were almost porcelain. Framed by the white straps of her garter belt, her posterior seemed to invite invasion. I looked over at the equally becoming, yet more mature, exposed rear globes of the stewardess. It was a pleasurable contrast in lustful choices, the tight, virginal looking, exposed rear hole of Celine or the giving, easily penetrated but inevitably more dexterous nether entrance of the older woman. Natanya issued another soft toned 'suggestion' to her ward. "Celine, why don't you spread your thighs so that Mr. Harry can see your lovely quim. Arch your back and present it to him like a good little girl."

The slender, graceful girl edged her thighs apart and raised her rear. Presented were her delicate love lips covered with a moss of curly brown fur. The sight of her pubic growth, apparently untrimmed and left wild, was an incongruous juxtaposition to her pale skin and the whiteness that framed her body. It was like she had exposed her dirty, little secret, evidence of her womanly lusts amidst a patina of innocence.

I also could not help but notice that she lacked the angry red 'k' that appeared so brazenly on the buttock of the older woman. Apparently she had not been yet introduced into the full panoply of female slavery. Was there hope for her yet? Who could tell? But as long as she was able to keep her flesh intact, she would remain ostensively a free woman. She was imbonded, no doubt, in some way to the mysterious, amoral spider woman, but she was not yet property. Perhaps she would somehow escape that fate. I didn't know. But I did know that I would give my eye teeth for a chance to explore her tender flesh, to have her knelt over and supine on my bed, ready to encase my needy pole with her delectable crevasse.

There were a few moments of silence as Natanya allowed me to absorb the beauteous form of her charge. She seemed to be taunting me with her flesh. I wondered if she would allow me to sample it.

"Celine is quite pretty, isn't she, Harry," the woman finally spoke. "She's been with me for about six months now and she has yet to have her comely form pierced by a prick. I bought her from an orphanage in Bucharest on her eighteenth birthday. They had been saving her for a special buyer and had carefully preserved her innocence."

"It must have been a difficult exercise in restraint," I said. I had heard tales of the cruelties inflicted on the young girls in many former Eastern Block orphanages after the fall of the Soviet Union. They were often a breeding farm for prostitutes, young girls broken in and forced to service the staff of the institution before being sold off to pimps or exported to the West to work as street whores in London, Berlin or even New York. Someone had appreciated the value of Celine's delicate, fragile flesh and preserved her for just the right buyer. I wondered just what business Natanya was in. She answered my question without asking.

"I run a very special brothel in Paris, catering to the whims of wealthy female clients. Celine has turned into one of the favorites. She can spend hours pleasuring a cunt and when she comes her whole body quivers and shakes like she is giving up her soul. I've had several offers from women who wanted to penetrate her, but I wanted to save her for something special. She's one in a million."

"I'd say," I agreed. Apparently, I was not to get the chance to fuck the pretty, little wastrel. How much more enticing is the morsel that we cannot have. My cock had hardened at the thought of feeling her soft skin against mine. I felt it pressing against the seam of my jockeys and I had to squirm in my seat to give it free rein.

"But enough about that, Harry," Natanya continued. "Let me tell you where we're going. I've been commissioned by our fat friend to obtain for him an item of very precious value. It's something I learned about from a very well connected and extremely wealthy client of mine. We will be landing in about five hours in the northern part of Pakistan. From there we will proceed deep into the Hindu Kush, the mountainous north. There's a monastery there where we will turn over the gold and receive the item that I'm discussing. Your job will be to guard the gold and make sure that we get in and get out without incident. My father was Pakistani and my mother was Russian. I speak Urdu and I'll do all the talking. You just keep that cannon you keep under your jacket handy."

"Pakistan?" I asked, incredulous.

"Well, where we're going its not so clear if it's Pakistan, China or India, the border gets kind of mixed up up there. The monastery has been in existence for about eight hundred years. We'll travel by SUV at first for the first fifty miles and then by pack animal for the last twenty. But up there, twenty miles will take us a few days. So I hope you like the great outdoors."

As a matter a fact, I always hated camping out as a kid. My Dad, for the brief times he was home from prison, would take me and my two younger brothers up to the Delaware Water Gap in Jersey where we would suffer through the miseries of camping out. We had a beat up old tent and some sleeping bags and every time we went it seemed like it would rain. My father would bring a case of beer and some hot dogs and we would watch him drink himself into oblivion. Not happy times. I didn't relish the idea of sleeping under the big sky of the Hindu Kush, whatever that was. But a job was a job.

The flight was long and uneventful. I shut off the chit chat with Natanya by taking a nap. When I awoke, the stewardess got up and served us lunch, a microwaved atrocity that pretended to be some kind of beef bourguignon. There was a very nice Merlot served with it. Natanya allowed Celine to come and kneel by her feet while she served her small forkfuls from her own plate. Watching the girl's lips work over her meal, eyeing her delectable form and her pretty, white dress, I could not help but bring into my mind the moss covered, unexplored sex that she was hiding beneath it.

I spent the rest of the time looking out the window at the vast expanse of Africa as we jetted across it and then the silvery, glittering surface of the Indian Ocean. My cock was in dire need of servicing but I still didn't want to exhibit my lusts in front of the jaded, cold spider woman. It was she, however that broke the ice.

The slave girl/stewardess had just finished serving me a glass of gin and tonic with a bright green wedge of lime squeezed into it when Natanya spoke to her.

"Slut, Mr. Harry has been very patiently waiting for you to suck his cock. I want you to kneel down and unzip him and take his cock in your mouth."

The slave girl looked at me for permission. It was undoubtedly strange for her to be taking orders from a woman, particularly as they pertained to a male master. I hesitated for a moment, considered my pride, and then the thought of having her succulent lips around my pole won out.

The naked, buxom, shapely woman knelt gracefully between my thighs and reached for the zipper for my pants. I arched my hips to give her some help and she soon had my solidified wand in her palm, stroking it prefatory to consuming it between her lips. I noticed Celine kneeling by her mistress's knees and watching. Natanya was stroking her hair softly. "Celine never saw a man's cock until yesterday. The sight of your dangling meat quite excited her. She's going to have to learn to suck a cock someday so I want her to watch a professional at work."

"Ungh," I just commented as the slave girl took my tool between her lips and applied her moist heat to it. I had never perfected the art of maintaining a conversation while my cock was sucked and I didn't want to practice now. As the slave girl slowly and expertly drew her lips up and down my stiffened pole, I gave out a sigh of satisfaction.

"See how she works it with her lips, Celine," Natanya was telling her ward. "Inside her mouth, she's stroking Harry's cock with her tongue. You have to patient and attentive to give a good blow job."

My eyes had focused on the lovely face of the young girl. Her pale, narrow lips were parted and her gaze drifted back and forth from the activities of the slave girl in my lap and my own face.

"See how Harry enjoys it, Celine," Natanya continued. "Why don't you let him look at your tits while he gets ready to come? He'll really like that, wouldn't you, Harry?"

I gave a grunt of approval as I absorbed the pleasurable efforts of the slave girl between my thighs. Celine unbuttoned the front of her lacy, white party dress and pulled it down over her soft, round shoulders. She wore a smooth, silk bra, white like her dress, that held her round, full breasts firmly. She unfastened the clasp that held it together between her breasts and let them fall free. They were heavy for so slender a girl, but not disproportionally large. They were as pale as her rump had been, but tinted with a slight pink. Her nipples were flat and wide and her areolas were dark, like little chocolate cookies on her breasts. The sight of her womanly prizes triggered my orgasm and I grunted and groaned as I pumped the product of my loins into the slave girl's mouth. When I was done, the slave girl conscientiously sucked down the last few drops of come from the tip of my cock and then folded its softening presence back into my pants.

We landed near a small city called Gilgit, a dusty, dirty, thriving border town. The heat of the place slapped me in the face as I emerged from the plane. Klitzman's island was hot, but it was not like this. It seemed like the place had never had a cool breeze for a thousand years. In the winters, I discovered later, the place got quite cold and the snow sometimes piled up very high. But you couldn't tell that from where I was standing.

There was a long, black limo waiting for us when we descended the stairs from the plane. The driver, a thin, almost emaciated Pakistani with short, black hair, a deep brown complexion and wearing a white shirt, narrow black tie and a wrinkled, black suit two sizes too small for him popped the trunk and then jumped out and opened the rear door. I was carrying my heavy, black valise and my canvas bag. Natanya was carrying a stylish, leather bag. I took it from her and I threw the bags into the trunk and climbed into the limo, placing the valuable valise at my feet. The women had preceded me and I slid in next to Celine. The door slammed shut and we drove off. No customs, no immigration, no cops. Nothing.

The cool air of the limo soon refreshed me. We rode in silence, the long, sleek, black car piercing the tight, crowded streets of the city. I could feel Celine's warm thigh next to mine and I remembered the sight of her lovely, youthful breasts from a few hours before, not to mention the dark treasure between her thighs. I tried to put them out of my mind as the car sped along.

We stopped in the courtyard of a modern looking hotel. It was several stories high and a mixture of glass and steel. The driver brought our bags in and, after checking in, two adjoining rooms with double beds, we went up to our rooms. Natanya had a little giggle when I presented my passport to the hotel clerk, a slender Pakistani woman with a colorful sari draped around her shapely body, a diamond implanted in the side of her nose. "Thank you, Mr. Lime," she said as I handed over the cash for our bill.

"Lime?" Natanya giggled. "Harry Lime?" I looked at her disconcertedly. I didn't like being made fun of.

"Someone has made a joke for you, Harry. Don't you get it? Harry Lime? The movie, *The Third Man*? Orson Wells?" She could barely hold in her mirth.

"Never caught it," I said, deadpan. I made a vow to watch it when I got back to the island and to break somebody's neck if I didn't like what I saw.

Natanya continued to giggle as we ascended the elevator. I watched as she and the girl went into their room and then went into mine.

There was nothing to do for the rest of the day. Natanya had made arrangements for a driver to take us north in the morning. It was late in the afternoon, and I was hungry, but I didn't want to take the chance of leaving the hotel with my fortune in gold. I had heard stories about these frontier cities in Southwest Asia. The city was undoubtedly a main transit point for the heroin trade. Also, terrorists, revolutionaries, smugglers and corrupt governmental types probably swarmed the city. I wasn't here as a tourist and so I decided to stay in my room. I had advised Natanya to do the same.

I ordered up a curried stew from room service and when the bellboy brought it made arrangements for him to bring me a bottle of gin, ice and some tonic. I knew that he would have to get it from the black market. Sure enough, about an hour later he knocked on my door and produced a bottle of Gilby's. Not my first choice, but I was roughing it after all. It cost me a hundred bucks.

The tonic and gin soothed me as I lay on my bed. The valise was under my pillow and my .45 was on the bed beside me. The television was on and I was watching a soccer match between Sri Lanka and Malaysia. I had gone through the three other channels showing a Pakistani soap opera, a dubbed American Western and some kind of weird game show. At least I could follow the soccer match. When it ended tied 2-2, I turned back to the channel with the western and there was some Hong Kong gangster flick on.

After my second gin, I decided to get another look at the small fortune I was carrying. I opened the case on the bed in front of me and gazed at the glittering coins. I knew that I could slip out of the hotel in a moment. A few hundred bucks would probably get me a car and a driver. I could be gone for almost twelve hours before I was missed. With a little more baksheesh spread around, I could be on some tropical Pacific isle within a day or so. But what then? It would be a toss up as to who would find me first, Bederson's boys or Klitzman's. I would put my money on Klitzman's since they at least knew that I was out and around. But then Bederson might have some other inside man at Klitzman's and he might find out that I had slipped my leash and where to start looking for me. I might have a good few months at best. Then I would be dog meat. No, I was stuck with the cards that fate had dealt me. I closed the valise and put it back under my pillow.

Around eight o'clock that night, I heard some voices in the hallway. They were distinctly American. I stepped to my door and could hear a young woman complaining to a male companion. "What the fuck are we doing here?" she said somewhat drunkenly. "This place sucks!"

An idea sprung into my head. I had been looking for a way to contact Bederson. All I had was an 800 number given to me by one of his female agents who had been captured and enslaved by Klitzman's minions. She was supposed to have been my contact with Bederson but she and her female friend had been snatched. Although she had been suspected of being a spy, she had suffered Rukimo's not delicate interrogation without spilling the beans. She had revealed herself to me one day after I had saved her from being tossed into the Atlantic as shark food. I hadn't known that she was my contact and she surprised me later after I had fucked her. Later, before I had had her sold to a Mexican drug smuggler at her request so that she might try and escape and get back to the States, a project that sounded very doubtful at best to me, she had given me the 800 number, the only information that she had for me.

I opened my door, my .45 carefully hidden behind my back and I got just a glimpse of the American couple as they entered their room and shut the door behind them. The girl was thin with mousy, long brown hair, dressed in a flowing, multicolored, long skirt, probably of Indian origin and a rust colored peasant blouse. The man had dirty, long blond hair, looked abut 25 or so and was wearing blue jeans and a black Rolling Stones t-shirt with a pair of gaping, toothy, red lips on it. If they had a cell phone I could call Bederson and find out what the fuck I was supposed to be doing. Maybe, just maybe, he would get me out of Klitzman's clutches.

I put the .45 in the back of my waistband, untucked my shirt to cover it and then knocked on the American couple's door. The guy opened it. He had a scraggly beard that covered most of his face. His eyes were red rimmed like he had been partaking of some of the local dope. He looked at me quizzically. "Who the fuck is it?" I heard the girl screech from inside the room. The guy turned back to her.

"Give me a fucking second, willya!" he yelled back. I didn't know if Natanya could hear from inside her room but things were not going well so far. I tried to put on my most obsequious demeanor, a tough thing to do when you look like me.

"I'm sorry to disturb you," I said sweetly. "I heard your voices and figured you were fellow Americans. I'm in a bit of a jam and I need to ask a favor."

"What kind of a favor?" the man asked. He face telegraphed that he was not in the most gregarious mood.

"Can I come in for a moment?" I replied. "I don't want to talk about it in the hallway. I'll make it worth your while, I promise."

The thought of money made the man's eyes light up. "Sure," he said smiling. "Come on in."

He opened the door and let me slide in past him. The bed was covered with dirty clothes and the sheets were mangled on the bed as if they couple had spent the afternoon fucking. The bathroom door was open and a moment later the girl came walking out. She had shed her skirt and was dressed in a pair of white panties. I could see her wild, untrimmed brown bush right through them. Unfortunately, she had left her blouse on so I didn't get a peak at what looked like bodacious tits.

"What the fuck?" the girl exclaimed. "Can't you see I'm half naked?" she screamed at the guy.

"Shut the fuck up," the man answered her. "It's business."

Despite her stated dismay at being seen in her undies, the girl flopped herself down on the bed and used the remote to turn on the TV. She settled on a kung fu movie.

"Okay, what's up," the man asked.

"You see," I said, "I'm on a business trip and my cell phone has died. I need to make a call, a private call, if you know what I mean, and I want to know if I can borrow your cell phone. You do have one, don't you?"

"Yeah, I have one," the youth replied. "But why should I let you make some drug deal on my phone? I don't want to end up in some shithole jail waiting for them to chop my hands off or something."

"Oh. It's not a drug deal, I can assure you," I answered him. I tried to think quickly. "I'm in textiles," I spat out. "I'm negotiating a contract with a local mill and I need to talk to my boss back in the States. I don't want to talk on the local phones because the owners of the mill are very well connected and are probably having the phones tapped. It's an 800 number so it won't cost you anything. And I'll pay you $100."

"A hundred bucks, eh," the man murmured. I could see him mulling it over. I knew he would say yes, it was just a matter of the price. Little did he know that I would have paid him ten grand.

"I'll make it two hundred," I said. "But I'll have to take the phone back to my room. It's a very private call."

The girl on the bed had been listening in while immersed in her movie. "Jesus Christ, Jeremy!" she yelled out. "You don't know this guy. He could be CIA or some shit like that. You could get us all murdered or something. Tell him to fuck off!"

The thought of having this broad bent over a rail and beating her with a riding crop crossed my mind. But the prospect of easy money had won the day.

"Shut the fuck up and mind your own business, Liz," he spat out back at her. He looked back at me. "Sure," he said.

I gave him the two hundred and he handed me his cell phone. Telling him that I would be back in a few minutes, I crept back across the hall to my room. My heart was pounding as I closed the door. If any of Klitzman's boys found out that I was making this phone call I would be chopped up into little pieces and sold as fish food. But I had to do it. If I didn't, then I might as well concede my soul as doomed. What excuse did I have for the life I was leading, the misery I brought to the unfortunate females back on the island if I punked out now? How could I justify as the lesser of two evils the cruel beating I had administered to the dismally unfortunate brunette the day before unless I was willing to act to bring about the greater good, the destruction of Klitzman's empire? I had to make the call.

I walked over to my bed stand and took a long pull on the gin, direct from the bottle, letting its fiery heat bring me courage. I then dialed the ten numbers Brenda, my prior sole contact with Bederson, had given me. The phone rang and a voice came on the line repeating the number that I had just dialed.

"My name is…." I started to say.

"Hold on please," the man's vice interrupted. There was about a minute of silence and then a familiar voice came on the line.

"Harry! We thought that you were dead!" It was Bederson. I wondered how they had got him so quickly but then that's what they did, wasn't it? The 800 number had probably been reserved exclusively for my call, if I ever got around to making it.

"Yeah, I'm alive," I answered. "No thanks to you."

"Getting plenty of pussy?"

Bederson hadn't told me what life with Klitzman would be like. He probably knew that either 1) I wouldn't believe him; or 2) I would have balked at being his rat fink. I didn't blame him really. But all I wanted now was out.

"You've got to get me out of this," I told him. I didn't need to answer his question. I was sure he knew the answer to that.

"You're job's not done, Harry."

"What job? All your little friend told me was to keep my eyes open and remember who I saw. Some big shot apparently supposed to be Klitzman's mole or something in the government. I don't even know who I'm looking for."

"Harry, where are you? Where did you get this phone?" When you don't want to answer a question, ask one back.

"I'm in fucking Pakistan!" I yelled. I related to him how I had conned the American kid out of his phone and what I knew about my mission.

"You're on a mission for Klitzman?"

"Yeah, a mission for Klitzman.," I replied angrily. "And I want to get out now. I'll tell you everything I've learned, everyone I've seen. You could take him down in a minute!"

"Sorry, Harry. Not yet."

"When?" I asked, my voice tense with frustration and anger. "When?"

"When we decide, Harry. Or do you want to go back to Atlanta? Maybe this time we'll send you to Marion, you know, the super max. You can come out of your cell once every few days for an hour and walk around the exercise yard by yourself. You could see if you could break the world record for jacking off in a day. Would you like that?"

I knew all about the super max: solitary confinement, no privileges, no contact with the outside. Years of bitter loneliness and then death. I didn't want that at all.

"No," I replied morosely.

"Then keep doing what you're doing. Report when you can so we know that you're alive. Have fun."

I thought of all the cunts that I had plowed over the last many months, the *haute cuisine* that I had consumed, my little Carol who was hopefully going to be mine again when I returned to Klitzman's Isle. But then death lurked at my door every minute of every day. It was clear that Bederson would be of no help. I was trapped. It was a gilded cage all right, but it was a cage nonetheless.

"All right," I answered. "But don't take too long. If these guys guess that I'm a rat, they'll peel my skin off of my body."

"I'll keep that in mind, Harry," Bederson answered. I could tell from his voice that he wouldn't. Then I told him all about Brenda, the name of the drug lord who had bought her, the general location of his hacienda in Mexico. If they didn't wait too long, before she was discarded as being all used up a whore, they could save her.

"We'll do what we can, Harry," Bederson answered.

"You need to do more than that, Bederson," I shot back at him. "She's one of your own and she's in a living hell. This guy who bought her is really nasty."

"Listen, Harry, Brenda knew what she was risking. I can't jeopardize the whole operation for her sake. You know what evil Klitzman is doing. Think of all the young girls that he kidnaps and enslaves, the shit he does all over the world. Brenda's well being doesn't compare to all of that. I said we'll do what we can. I know the fellow you're talking about. If the timing is right, I might be able to get the Federales to raid his place. But on our time, not yours."

I realized that I had done all I could for the unfortunate Brenda. Maybe she could be saved, maybe not. It was not my problem. I had done all that I could.

"Listen," Bederson continued, "I have the trace on that phone. You made a serious breech of security involving these kids. I'm going to have them picked up later tonight as terrorists. They'll be out of circulation for a long while so don't worry about it."

I felt a deep pang of regret that I had involved the young American couple. Instead of doing good, I kept on causing harm. I thought of trying to talk Bederson out of it but then gave it up. He wouldn't have listened to me anyway.

"Good luck, Harry," he said finally. "And keep in touch."

CHAPTER SIX

I brought the phone back to the unsuspecting young couple. Liz was still sitting on the bed. Jeremy asked me if I wanted to smoke some hash. "Primo from Afghanistan," he said. I declined respectfully and retreated to my room. Later that night, I heard their door broken down and a lot of shouting. They were gone in the morning.

Just about when I was going to retire, I heard a tapping on my door. I grabbed the .45 and stood next to it and asked who was there. I heard Natanya's voice on the other side. "Open up, Harry, I've got a surprise for you."

I opened the door cautiously and saw her standing there with two, young Pakistani girls next to her. They were dressed in long, flowing, red robes and had shawls over their heads partially obscuring their faces.

"What the fuck are you doing out," I asked the spider woman angrily. She was supposed to stay in for the night.

"Oh, I thought I'd like to sample the local talent, Harry. I got one for you too. Which one do you want?"

It was true that she could have been out hunting pussy, but why do that when she had her own private lap slut in her room? She could have been out doing anything. But then why would she advertise the fact that she had been out by bringing back these two whores? I wavered for a moment while I took in the girls' shapely forms. I was pretty used to having a fuck buddy for the night and Celine's presence in the limo next to me had gotten me pretty riled up, something I hadn't gotten over even though it was hours later. The girl on the right looked up at me with her large, brown eyes. She was pretty. She had a diamond lodged in her nose like the girl downstairs did. She looked young, but over the legal age. I surely didn't want to get busted for child molestation in Pakistan. I wouldn't have to worry about Klitzman or Bederson then. The other girl was pretty too, but there was something about the first one that appealed to me. Her smile was just a little bit comelier, her hips seemed a little more graceful, even through her robes. "Okay," I said, pointing to her with the .45. "I'll take this one.

There was nothing on TV anyway. The girl quickly stripped and jumped onto the bed. Her brown skin was clean and smooth. She had dark, broad eyebrows and a long, narrow nose. Her lips, which were wide and plump, were covered with a purplish lipstick. And she had large, pleasing breasts, deep, dark areolas sitting on plump, brown mounds of pleasure.

I spent about two hours fucking her, or, should I say, she spent two hours fucking me. Her body was sinewy and pliant and she slithered beneath me as I stroked my hardness in her plush, agile furrow. She used her pussy's walls like a hand as she caressed my manhood each time I drew my stroke backwards. I came mightily, groaning with pleasure as her brown hands, topped off with purple polish on her long, pointy nails, caressed and stroked my back. It was unusual to be fucking a woman who was not a slave, at least not in the literal sense. I was sure that she served some Pakistani pimp who had probably bought her from her parents so that they could eat and feed the rest of the family for the coming year. But she failed to exhibit any sorrow or reticence at her profession and laughed joyfully when my cock rose to attention for the third time. She sucked my dick skillfully for what seemed to be almost an hour before she let me come.

I didn't want to send her home for the night in case she reported to her pimp about the rich Americans in the hotel and he came back to rob me. But I didn't want her wandering around the room while I slept. She had been wearing a long, silken scarf when she came into the room and I used it to bind her wrists behind her back and then took my belt and secured her pretty, long legs. She seemed frightened at first when I went to bind her. As far as I could tell, she didn't speak a word of English. But I calmed her by stroking her long, black hair and purring soothing words to her.

She was there lying next to me in the morning, awaiting my pleasure. I had left a wake up call for 6:30 so that I could shower and shave before we went on our trek to the high mountains of the Hindu Kush. I released her and let her go pee. When she returned, she pointed to the bed expectantly. I shook my head 'no'. She gave a little, disappointed smile and then began to dress. When she was done I handed her a $100 bill. It was the only money I had and I didn't want her to walk out empty handed. I sure hoped that Anthony didn't expect receipts. With the price of the hotel rooms, I had gone through $500 bucks already. She looked at the bill, astounded. It was probably more money than she saw in a year. She pointed to the bed and began to undress all over again. I shook my head and, grabbing her, eased her towards the door and pushed her out of the room.

I showered and shaved quickly, keeping the valise and my peacemaker near me at all times. I decided to wear the pastel pink polo shirt that had been provided me and I dressed, packed up my things and left the room.

When I knocked on Natanya's door there was, at first, no answer. I could hear some strong, feminine moaning through the thin door. I was about to walk away when the door opened. It was Natanya and she was stark naked. I was surprised, to say the least. She smiled at me gracefully as if nudity was her natural state and urged me into her room.

"Good morning, Harry," she said pleasantly. Her breasts were sharp and heavy on her chest. Her black bush was wiry and spread widely over her loins. Her thighs were firm and long. My cock began to tingle.

The noise that I had heard emanated from the pretty Celine. She was sitting at the head of the bed, her hands tied above her to the headboard, her ankles bound by her stockings from yesterday and affixed to the headboard on either side of her head. The brown skinned whore that I had rejected last night was naked and kneeling between Celine's pale, white thighs and she was administering oral delight to the bound girl's moss covered pussy. The whore's ass was in the air and I could see her black hair covered mons glistening between her thighs.

Celine was moaning with enforced delight. Her child like face was tinted a bright red from her passion and distorted from her lust. Natanya strolled leisurely over to the bed and sat next to her, stroking her long, thin, brown hair.

"Celine is getting her morning relief, Harry. It'll be just a few more minutes. Wait till you see her come."

I put down my valise and bag and stood there, marveling at the delectable sight of the young girl in passion. Her breasts heaved on her chest and her thighs were quivering. The girl looked at me with her big, brown eyes as she struggled to withstand the oral caresses to her loins. Her lips were pursed tight and she was emitting long, deep moans as her crisis approached. I had little idea what the poor girl thought about all of this, the trip to Pakistan, her brief sojourn to Klitzman's domain, me. I surmised that the spider woman's hold on her was a threat to send her back to the cruel overseers of her Hungarian orphanage for corrective measures. Was her fate as the plaything of rich, Western European women worse than being a street whore or a slut in some low life brothel somewhere? I doubted it. But it surely wasn't a fate that she preferred. Her whole demeanor bespoke her unhappiness at her current life style.

But right now, she looked like she was having a world class orgasm, and that couldn't be all bad. As her lusts climbed, her cheeks bulged out and the redness in her face deepened. Natanya was caressing her pretty, youthful breasts, tugging on the little nipples, pinching and mauling her firm, succulent mounds. The girl's eyes rolled up and her body gave a sudden jerk. "Ohhhhhhhh!" she moaned. "Ohhhhhhhhh! Ahhhhhhhhrgh, Ahhhhhhhrgh Ahhhhhhhrgh!" as she came. Nantanya had described her as looking like she was giving up her soul when she orgasmed and I could see what she meant. They were the first sounds I had heard from her mouth, not even a "Yes, mistress," or a "No, mistress." Her limbs fought mightily at her bonds and her whole body shook. The native girl between her thighs continued her merciless attentions to her sex, bobbing her head up and down as she licked her expert tongue the length of the young girl's slit, sucking hard at the nub of pleasure at its top.

The echoing of the girl's moans and screams of pleasure throughout the small room shortly began to subside. Her body was covered by a patina of sweat and her lovely face softened as her crisis passed. The Pakistani girl raised her head from her loins and looked to Natanya for approval. Natanya said something to her in her native tongue and the girl withdrew from between Celine's tender, upraised thighs and rose from the bed. She placed her hands together in front of her and gave the spider woman a little bow. Natanya, having risen to her feet gave a similar signal back. The girl, giving me a sly, comely look, dressed quickly and left. I saw no cash exchanged between them.

I was still standing near the door, mesmerized by what I had witnessed. Natanya had returned to the bed and was giving Celine's moist, dilated quim a tender caress. My cock was as hard as a fist. I wanted nothing more than to climb up on the bed and initiate the lovely, prostrate girl into the rigors of fucking. Why the spider woman was tantalizing me with the girl's flesh I did not know. But whatever her scheme was, it was working.

Natanya leaned over to the girl and took possession of her lips while her hand probed her loins. She broke the kiss and then caressed Celine's long, chestnut colored hair. "You're a good little slut, Celine," she said.

The older woman unfastened Celine's hands and ankles from the bed and then pulled her to her feet. "I'm going to take a quick shower, Celine. You've gotten Mr. Harry all hot and bothered. I want you to give him a nice blow job while I wash up, okay?"

The girl looked over at me apprehensively. She was about to embark on a whole new level of degradation, being a plaything for men as well as women. I had guessed by now that the young girl had been forbidden all manner of speech by her mistress. Natanya gave Celine's breast a little tweak and then walked into the bathroom.

I stood there astounded at the spider woman's instructions to the virginal, young girl. I wondered what kind of a web she was spinning for me, but I wasn't about to pass up the chance to have the delectable girl's sweet lips around my crank. I lowered my fly and sat down on a chair that stood on the side of the room next to the bed. My cock was already hard and I had to struggle to get it out from my jockey's. I spread my thighs invitingly. The girl gave a deep, forlorn sigh accompanied by a pathetic, little frown. She looked beautiful as the early morning light from the sliding doors that led to the small patio outside the room struck her body, giving her a luster and glow. She gave a quick, angry glance at the door to the bathroom, as if casting a curse on her mistress, and then dutifully advanced towards me, her breasts shivering slightly as she walked.

Gracefully, the naked, young girl knelt between my thighs and then gingerly took my hardened shaft in her right hand. Looking up at me one last time before her ordeal began, her eyes brimming with tears, she then lowered her thin lips to my shaft and subsumed it within.

It was like a dream come true. The girl slid her lips slowly down my pole giving it a gentle, careful suck. My mind reeled with the effects of her moist heat on my prick. I looked down and watched as her lips slid up again, her tongue swirling around my tool. The sight of my manhood slithering in and out of her dainty mouth was exhilarating.

The girl held on to the base of my cock as she slid her lips slowly up and down its surface. Each time that she descended upon it, I could see the slight bulge in her cheeks that my occupation of her oral cavity caused. Her left hand was resting gently on my right thigh as she worked to drive my lusts. I took hold of the small, dainty right hand that circled my cock and pulled it away, leaving only her mouth to service me. As she sucked my wand, bringing wave after wave of excitement to my cock, I softly stroked her smooth, thin, long brown hair. My passion built with each hesitant, but surprisingly skillful, caress of my pole with her lips.

When my tool began its dance of joy, the girl pulled her head back as if in surprise. I held her steady with my hand, forcing her to drink of my essence. As she gurgled and coughed, my cock shot load after load of my steamy white cum into her mouth. I groaned with pleasure at each spurt until my forces were exhausted.

Natanya had emerged from the bathroom, rubbing a large, fluffy, white towel across her nubile body.

"Don't spill any of Mr. Harry's spunk on his pants, Celine," she called out to the girl mirthfully. "Drink it all down."

Celine slurped as she tried to maintain my jizz in her mouth as my cock softened within it. I removed my hands from her head and she lifted it up, letting my cock slide free. She looked up at me dolefully and then at her mistress. Her face was contorted as if she had just been given a spoonful of castor oil. She was clearly disconcerted at the prospect of swallowing her first load of man juice, but after a moment of indecision, weighing whether to suffer the fate worse than death or her mistress's displeasure, I saw her throat flex and knew that my load had passed into her belly.

The women dressed while I sat in the chair watching them, trying to be nonchalant. The spider woman readorned herself all in black and then drew a brush through her long, straight, black hair, which was still wet, until in ran clear and smooth. "No shower for you today, Celine," she told the naked girl who had been standing there watching her mistress dress. "We're in a hurry to get going. But I bought a pretty, new dress for you to wear today and some nice sandals."

Natanya drew from the closet a bright yellow dress and presented it to the girl. Celine looked at it for a moment and then took it from the hanger, drew it over her head and let it slide down her beauteous body. No undies today either, I figured. The dress had a deep, curved neckline that showed off the tops of her firm, youthful breasts to great advantage. The waist was tight and the skirt had wide pleats that caused it to flow out from her body. It reached to just below her knees, modest and yet tantalizing when you thought of her nakedness underneath it. Natanya handed her a pair of leather sandals that strapped around her ankles giving her lower limbs an aura of confinement. The bodice of the dress was supported by wide straps that circled around Celine's pale white neck and tied off behind her head. It would be a simple matter of loosening it so that her pretty breasts could feel the air.

Natanya packed up her suitcase and moments later we were ready to leave. "I told the driver to have some hot tea and something to eat for us so we can get on the road," she told me. I wondered what strange concoction these folks considered breakfast. I had been ready for a nice omelet and orange juice in the café downstairs. But who was I to argue? I wanted to get going too. The sooner that we got to where we were going the sooner I could unload my burden of gold. Carrying over three hundred thousand dollars around in this Wild West kind of town gave me the heebie jeebies.

Natanya wanted to take the elevator down to the ground level which led to the parking area of the hotel, but I told her that I wanted to take the stairs. Ever since I saw the *Godfather* I always had this lingering fear of someday having an elevator door open and being greeted by a shotgun blast. We would be sitting ducks as we emerged in the garage underneath the hotel. I didn't know if anyone knew what I was carrying, but, hey, why take the chance?

It was three flights down to the garage where our driver was waiting. As we emerged from the stairwell, I saw a small, brown skinned man dressed in blue jeans and a reddish brown t-shirt standing outside a gleaming, brand new Land Rover. He seemed surprised to see us emerge from the stairs rather than the elevator. I could see that the back of the Rover was crowded with all kinds of gear and I remembered that we were going to have to spend some nights under the stars on our journey. I shuddered when I thought of it.

The women proceeded ahead of me and I couldn't help watch Celine's lithe hips sway in her pretty, yellow frock as she walked. The memory of her lips around my willy wacker not more than a half hour ago was rolling through my mind. I know that I should have been scanning the garage for signs of trouble and, if I had, the appearance of two black haired, dark skinned men dressed in sneakers, blue jeans and t-shirts and wielding large, forbidding looking handguns would not have taken me by surprise. Thinking with my dick had always been one of my faults. "Here we go again," I thought.

I had just reached the outside of the Land Rover when the men appeared. It was much too late to draw my piece and all I could do was stand there like a stupid shit and gawk at the cannons in their hands. The men were grinning wildly at me, their eyes flickering between my resigned face and the black, leather valise I held in my left hand. For a few moments there was dead silence. All I could hear was the feint drone of the morning traffic above ground as it echoed through the confined space of the underground garage. "I'm dead," I thought. "Fuck!"

The man closest to me signaled with his gun that I should drop the valise on the ground. I dropped both it and the canvas bag that held my personals. The sound of the heavy valise falling resounded through the expansive, concrete underground. My back was up against the Land Rover and the driver stood to my right and the women to my left. I saw, out of the corner of my eye, the driver begin to edge away from me and, on the other side, Natanya drawing the shocked Celine out of the zone of danger.

Well, I thought, my last blow job was one of the best. That's the way it should be.

But it ain't over until the fat lady sings and the armed man who approached me obviously was no pro. His greed had gotten the better of him. He watched me warily as he approached to claim his prize, his gun pointed out at me in his right hand as he began to crouch over to reach down for the valise. He looked down for just an instant, making sure that he had a good grasp on its handle. It was then I made my move.

The man was about a foot away from me. I reached out with my left hand and grabbed his right wrist, forcing the hand that held the gun to point downwards. At the same time, I had sneaked my right hand into my pants pocket and retrieved the switchblade that Anthony had obtained for me at my insistence. It was close in work, my specialty. I clicked the blade free and as it unfolded, swung my hand upwards so that the point of the blade caught the very surprised man in the soft spot between his jaw and his throat. As I drove it into his brain, I twisted his body so that he was between me and the other gunman, shoving his dying body towards him. The other man's first shot hit his friend in the rear of his head, shooting blood and brains up into the air in a grotesque shower. The second shot caught him in the back, just below the left shoulder blade and passed through him. I felt the bullet graze my right arm as I scrunched behind the now dead man for protection.

Calmness in adversity is the ticket. A calm man will almost always prevail over an excited one. Not that my heart wasn't pounding in my chest or my brain buzzing with the thrill of sudden, lethal violence, but I kept my cool. The gunman who was shooting at me in a desperate effort to save his own life had taken two wild shots in his panic. The only two he was going to get.

I pushed the first man's lifeless body up against the gunman and drove him backwards. He retreated as his friend's bloody corpse was forced against him until his back struck one of the wide, concrete support columns that held up the ceiling of the garage. I could hear the air jetting out of him from the force of the collision. I had drawn the blade of my sticker from the first man's neck and now swung it behind his head, using all of the force that my arm would give me. The point of the blade entered the second man's head just above the left ear. There was a moment of tension as it worked its way through his thick cranial covering and then it slid in like slicing into cranberry sauce. The man gave a shriek and then his body collapsed.

I stood there for a moment, blood and brains dripping down my face and chest, as I took in the sight of the two dead men. Their crumpled bodies gave little twitches as their nerve endings surrendered to lifelessness. I hoped that they had said their prayers that morning to Allah or Vishnu or whoever they worshiped. They would be meeting him or her or it right now and they had better be ready for same fast talking.

It seemed much longer than it really was that I stood peering down at the ruined bodies. It was Celine's shrieks of horror that snapped me out of it. I dropped the shiv and turned immediately, the .45 in my hand, ready for the driver to take up where his compadres had failed. He was clearly in on it as had been given away by his look of surprise when we failed to exit the elevator. If we had, we would have undoubtedly been trapped. As it was, when we approached them from another direction, the stick up amateurs had probably wanted to get much closer before they blazed away at me.

The driver's brown skinned face was ashen as I walked quickly over to him, the .45 extended at the end of my arm.

"Get on the ground, motherfucker," I yelled at him. My voice boomed in the cavernous space. His body shook and he dropped to his knees and then his belly instantly.

"Please, no! Please don't kill me! Please! Please!" he screamed. Celine was still screeching in terror and revulsion at what she had just seen. I spun the .45 in her direction and shouted, "Shut the fuck up!" Her eyes widened and her voice went silent. I could see her frail body trembling. Natanya put her arm around her and comforted her, "There, there, sweetie, Harry's not going to shoot you. Are you, Harry?" she said looking at me intently. She was a cool one all right. I couldn't prove it, but I would lay ten to one that she had set up the whole thing. I added together her trip out the night before, the delay upstairs, making sure that my mind was on Celine's pussy and not my job. She had made a small protest when I told her we were taking the stairs, not insistent, and not remarkable at the time, but ominous now.

The hand holding the .45 was shaking wildly. It was covered with blood up to my elbow. My jacket was ruined, not to mention my pretty, pastel pink polo shirt. The gun was now aimed at the middle of Natanya's forehead. Anthony had warned me about her. If the stick up had been successful, she could have told Klitzman that I was a careless pussyhound and had fucked up and she would undoubtedly have walked away with a large part of the 300K. But I was just one shade short of being sure. And if I blew her away, I would have to do the driver and probably Celine too. And then I would be on the lam from the local fuzz and have an awful lot of 'splainin to do.

"Good job, Harry," Natanya said coolly. "But I'd appreciate it if you pointed that thing elsewhere."

I lowered my trembling hand and turned back to the driver. He was watching me with his head craned up, his whole body shaking with fear.

"Don't kill our driver, Harry," Natanya interjected. "We need him to take us where we're going."

"How do I know I can trust him," I said dully. I wasn't really going to argue. Killing wasn't something I did for sport. Business was business, but I took no joy in it. I was just looking for an excuse to let him live.

"You don't know that he was involved, Harry. These were just two dirt bags looking to score off some tourists. Besides, even if he was, I doubt that he'd try and pull anything now."

I had to agree with her. From now on, this guy wouldn't squeeze out a fart without permission.

The situation diffused, my body started to calm. The adrenaline rush had subsided and I felt weak and spent. I went over to my carry bag and opened it, careful not to drip any blood on it, and retrieved the half empty bottle of gin from the night before. The breakfast of champions. I took a long swig and then another. It felt good going down. It was good to be alive. How many chances was God going to give me, I wondered. Why am I so fucking lucky? I should be dead a dozen times by now. But here I was, alive and breathing.

Tranquility had returned to the garage. Celine's crying had wound down to a mild whimper. Natanya stepped up to me. "You're a fucking mess, Harry, but I have to hand it to you. Klitzman knew what he was doing when he picked you. Now, let's figure out how to clean you up and get out of here."

There was a hose along the far wall behind a big black Mercedes and I brought my two bags over to it and stripped off my clothes. When I was naked, I drenched myself with the freezing cold water. It was surprising to get cold water in the middle of this pan fried landscape, but I figured the hotel's well was probably tapped into an underground spring. It felt refreshing. I washed the blood off of my body, soaking my hair until I was sure that all the little brain parts were gone. I took the extra pair of pants, some clean jockey's and a pale blue shirt from the carry bag and donned them. When I was dressed, I dragged the two bodies behind the Mercedes so they wouldn't be found right away. I quickly went through their pockets finding small wads of the local currency in each of their pants, some identity papers and a handwritten note in what appeared to me to be Urdu, written in a practiced, feminine hand. I took the money and the note and put them in my pocket and then washed away the trail of blood and brains down a drain in the middle of the floor. After cleaning my pig sticker, I collected their firearms and placed them in my duffle bag. No sense letting them be found by some 14 year old who would then go out and hold up some coffee shop. I wrapped my bloody shirt and pants in my jacket and tossed them in the back of the Rover. I would get rid of them later at some distance from the crime scene. No sense leaving a calling card.

The diver was still lying on the floor where I had left him and I signaled him to get in and start the Rover. I let the women sit in the back and I sat next to him in the front. I didn't know if he spoke much English, but later, when he became disposable, I would find out and learn by hook or crook what the real dope was on our little escapade. If Natanya was involved, I wanted to know for sure.

CHAPTER SEVEN

It took us a good twenty minutes to clear ourselves from the tangle of haphazard, unruly traffic of the city. The driver, true to Natanya's word, had brought a thermos full of hot, heavy flavored tea and some pastries filled with some kind of meat for our breakfast. I figured that if the two men who I had killed had been successful, it would have them enjoying the hot, baked pastries and the tea while they rode somewhere with Natanya to make their split. I wondered if Natanya would have let them live out the day. Somehow I doubted it. I had noticed the little bulge in the small, black purse that she carried and assumed that she was packing.

Once we had breeched the outskirts of the town, the riding was clear sailing. The rode was paved and there was little traffic. We passed oxen pulling carts going either way, men on bicycles, groups of chador covered women following male pedestrians. After a couple of hours even they thinned out.

We stopped for lunch at a roadside stand eating grilled strips of what I assumed to be goat and rice. The stand had a soda machine and for twenty rupees I obtained a freezing cold can of orange soda. I'm not a natural conversationalist, but the morning's killings had cast a pall over even any routine chit chat. I'm sure the driver was wondering when I would have him step outside the car and kill him. I wondered myself, but I figured that I would answer that question when he got us where we were going. I kept the .45 loosely held in my right hand and resting on my lap as we drove. Occasionally, he would look over and take a glance at it, smile at me nervously and then shift his glance back at the road ahead.

The blacktop lasted for about five hours. We turned off onto a dirt road that got thinner and thinner and rougher and rougher as we went along. The large, craggy, snow covered Hindu Kush Mountains loomed off in the distance. The closer we got, the more foreboding they became. I found it hard to believe that I would soon be crawling along its ravines and pathways on top of some kind of pack horse.

After another couple of hours, the terrain began to become really rough. We were climbing steadily in elevation. We all got out to piss a couple of times and consumed some more of those pastry covered things that seemed to be a staple of the local diet. The Rover bounced and swayed as the road became a mere trail and then vanished altogether. We were rumbling along on very rough country. The Rover seemed to turn almost vertical at some points as it strained to climb what I would have thought to be impassable hills.

It was just about sundown when we came to a small assembly of stone buildings. They were covered with what looked like thatch roofs. At the sound of our engine, three people, a man and two women emerged from one of the buildings and started to walk towards us. The man was tall and broad shouldered. He had a heavily weather-beaten face and was dressed in tan, canvas pants and a coarse, white, cotton shirt. He was wearing a dirty, yellowed vest of sheepskin and a round, cloth hat the had flaps that covered his ears. He was not young and from his face he could have been anywhere from fifty to eighty years old. He had a thick, broad black moustache that curled at the ends.

The women were dressed in long, white shifts that covered them from their shoulders to the ground. They looked like they might have been sewn together from burlap bags and then bleached. They wore calico scarves on their heads which were tied around their necks. One was short and heavy and she looked like she was about sixty years old. The other was younger, maybe forty. They both had wide, Asiatic faces, definitely not Pakistanis. All three of the people wore heavy, brown, leather brogans on their feet. As they approached, a third woman, who from a distance looked a little more slender and perhaps younger than the other women, poked her head from one of the huts and then disappeared again.

The Rover pulled to a halt, its tires skidding on the stony soil. Natanya immediately jumped out and spoke some words in what I assumed to be Urdu to the main. He nodded noncommittally and waved us to follow him.

I made sure that the driver handed over the keys to the Rover before I got out. I didn't want him deciding to take off without us. He gave me a nervous, obsequious grin and got out the driver's side.

We formed a little parade as we followed the man to his hut. The wind had picked up and I felt a chill go through my bones. I hoped that I wasn't expected to go gallivanting through the mountains that towered over the little assembly of buildings in my polo shirt and slacks. I also didn't want to mess up my nice, hand tooled Italian shoes.

As we neared the hut, I saw that one of the other buildings was a kind of barn, with a large, weathered, wooden door with a plank across it holding it closed. There was a kind of lean-to next to it with about fifteen or twenty goats milling about within a fenced enclosure. The group of buildings sat upon a small plateau covered with scraggly grass and a few dwarfish trees. The main hut was round and the roof was conical with a cutout on the top where wisps of smoke from a fire within emerged only to be whisked away by the strong wind.

The hut was dimly lit by several oil lamps hanging from beams that ran across the ceiling. There was a large pot sitting on the fire and the woman I had seen from a distance was stirring a brownish mixture with a large wooden spoon. "Where the fuck am I?" I thought. "And what the fuck am I doing here?"

The man motioned for us all to take our seats around the fire. The floor of the hut was covered with a heavy, woven rug. One of the women handed out primitive wooden bowls and the younger woman proceeded to fill them with the gunk from the pot. The older, heavy set woman passed out small, round, flat loaves of bread. *Haute cuisine* in the Hindu Kush, I thought. The mixture was spicy as hell and I was happy when the old man passed around a couple of goatskins filled with some kind of fermented, milky liquid. It packed quite a punch and soon the edge of my tension at our primitive surroundings wore off.

While we were eating, Natanya kept up an animated conversation with the old man. The driver was sitting next to her and I realized that Natanya and the man were not speaking Urdu, but some other strange, local dialect as the Pakistani was looking at them quizzically. Finally, Natanya came over to where I was sitting and sat down next to me.

"The man's name is Kien Hou," she sad to me quietly. "He's what we would consider ethnic Chinese. His people have been pushed out of their native areas by the Han Chinese coming in from eastern China to settle the area. He's a smuggler and kind of a bandit. He will take us to the monastery, but not tomorrow. He says that there's a storm brewing in the mountains and we have to wait for it to pass.

Besides, and I think that this is more to the point, he's expecting a shipment tomorrow and he wants to wait."

"You mean we've got to sit around here all day tomorrow doing nothing?" I asked, incredulous. Things were getting worse by the minute.

"Well, Harry, unless you want to go find the monastery by yourself and carry all of our shit, we have to wait. Don't worry, I'm sure the old man will let you fuck one of his goats." The tall, slender, black clad woman laughed heartily at her own joke. She looked over at Celine who was sitting in her pretty, yellow dress on the other side of me with a look of befuddlement on her face. At least I knew where we were going and what we were doing. Natanya had made it a point not to speak about our mission in front of her and for some reason wanted her kept in the dark.

"Celine will be happy to keep practicing her blow jobs, won't you, Celine," the woman said loud enough now for the young girl to hear. Celine gave a little grimace, but said nothing in return.

"What are we going to do about the driver," I asked the spider woman. "I don't trust him. I took the keys to the Rover, but he might know how to hotwire it and take off. I don't want him on the trip to the monastery with us and I don't want to leave him here."

"I'll take care of it, Harry," she replied. She spat out some words to the old man and nodded towards the driver. The Pakistani gave a frightened look, realizing that she was talking about him. The old man gave a grunt and stood. He grabbed the Pakistani by the scruff of his neck and dragged him towards the door. The driver was startled by the man's sudden attack and gave out a scream.

"Please, mistress! Please!" was all he had the opportunity to say as he was hauled out the door. The large, wooden door slammed shut and a moment later I heard a short, anguished scream from outside. The old man came back in a few moments after that wiping a broad, wooden handled knife on his pants, cleaning it of the Pakistani's blood. So much for questioning him. If he had been in league with Natanya, which I was pretty sure that he was, I would never learn it from his lips now. I had given Natanya the excuse to silence him forever.

We spent the rest of the evening lolling around the hut. I took what was probably more than my fair share of the tart brew and was feeling tired and horny. The three women cleaned up while Natanya kept up an animated conversation with the old man punctuated by occasional laughter. The old man was smoking a pipe and the aroma of the tobacco in the small hut was pungent. Celine just sat and watched her mistress carefully, wary, I supposed, of what new degrading acts her mistress would demand of her.

As if on some prearranged signal, the old man and the two older women left the hut and the younger one began to prepare it for the night. Four thick blankets were laid on the floor. I decided that it was time to go outside and take a whizz.

The wind cut through me like a cold knife when I stepped outside. There was a heavy cloud cover and it was so dark that I decided I would only venture a few steps away from the hut, not wanting to step on the body of the dead driver. As I let a long, steady stream of piss flow from my cock, I noticed that the barn door was ajar and I could see a feint light from within it. I guessed that the man and the two women were feeding their stock and bedding them down. Natanya came out with Celine in tow and took her a few feet away from the hut so that she could relieve herself before going to bed. I thought about her promise, or threat, depending upon your point of view, of more blow jobs from the delicate, young girl. When I tucked away my little friend, he had grown semi-hard at the memory of the girl's pretty, thin lips and agile tongue.

I went back inside the hut and the younger woman was lying down on one of the blankets that she had laid down and had drawn another one over her. Her shift and scarf was piled next to it. Her bare shoulders were exposed over the blanket and she was smiling strangely at me. I ignored her and took another pull of the hearty liquor from one of the goatskins and sat down pending instructions on where I should sleep.

Natanya brought Celine back in and had her strip and lay down on one of the blankets. She quickly drew off her trademark black clothes and got ready to join her sexual servant.

"Hey," I called out to her. "Where do I sleep?"

The tall, naked, black haired woman laughed. "You have the honor of sleeping with Fio, Mr. Kien's number three wife. I told Kien all about your escapade at the hotel and he was very impressed with your knife work. As his guest, you get to sleep with his wife." Natanya laughed again. "Enjoy," she added merrily and scooted down to the blanket where her naked ward was awaiting her. She pulled the top blanket over them and I could hear the young girl's gentle moan as their bodies joined.

I looked over at Fio, who was still eyeing me with a mischievous look. I didn't know whether Natanya was fucking with me or not. It did look like the young woman expected me to jump in the sheets with her, but, remembering the wide, bloody blade he carried, I decided to await a more definite invitation from the old man.

I could hear Natanya and Celine's sounds of love as I watched their bodies twist and turn under the blanket that covered them. I imagined my hands on the doll like, young body and my cock grew hard and needy. I also could not bar from my mind the lithe form of the spider woman, her enticing breasts and taut, sloping belly that led down to her love lips. Celine was in the middle of groaning her pleasure into the small hut when the old man and the other two women came back. The older one began to move around the hut extinguishing the oil lamps while the man drew off his vest and shirt and tossed them on the floor. The middle wife stripped as well and, giving me a lascivious leer, climbed onto the blanket near the door. The old man gave me a look, seemingly surprised that I was not yet busily rutting with his wife. I gave him a nod and then stood, releasing my belt and pulling my pants and shorts to my ankles. I kicked off my shoes and stepped out of my pants and then pulled my pastel blue shirt over my head. I stepped over to the blanket where Fio was waiting for me and took another look at the old man. He gave me an encouraging grin and I nodded back to him politely. I then crouched down and slid under the blanket.

The body of the Chinese woman was hot and smooth as our flesh connected. She gave a little sigh of pleasure as she put her strong arms around me and drew me against her. Wife number one, the senior of the three Asian women, must have extinguished the remaining lamp since the room was plunged into darkness. All that was left was a dull, reddish glow from the fire in the middle of the room. My companion slid her hands down my body as I lay on my side against her and circled my already rock hard cock and gave it a pleasurable squeeze. She had shifted to her side to face me and I could feel her stiff nipples against my chest and the exciting pressure of her soft, heavy breasts press into me. Her thick, hot lips wandered along my shoulder and neck and then up and over my chin until they found mine.

Her mouth was plush and hot as she drew my tongue inside it. Her hips rotated slowly against me and she placed my cock between our bellies and rubbed against it, causing me to sigh with pleasure. I could still hear the sounds of female lust emanating from Natanya and her little whore, sounds which were soon joined by the unmistakable noises of the old man and his middle wife engaged in a frenetic coupling. Fio placed her hands on my shoulders and forced me gently to my back. Our lips parted and she began to drag hers slowly and languorously down my neck, across my muscled chest and over my hard belly. Her hands played across my skin, complementing the excitement caused by her broad, warm lips. When she reached my loins, she took hold of my cock with her hands and then sucked it into her mouth.

I groaned with lust as her thick lips scoured my sturdy pole. I could feel her long, black hair laying across my belly and thighs. She worked my tool slowly and expertly, running her tongue along the bottom of my cock's plump helmet and then swirling it around the shaft as her mouth descended along its length.

I don't know how long she continued to torment my tool. My mind was hazy from the milky liquor I had drank and the sounds of the others fucking in the small confinement of the hut, mere feet away from me, made my body's trembling acceptance of the delights of Fio's mouth seem almost surreal. She brought me to the edge of climax twice. My hands gripped her head as it bobbed over my cock. I felt her lips leave me and her body begin to slide upwards. She dragged her full, lust hardened breasts along my torso and then she was atop of me. Deftly taking hold of my Peter and, after sliding it along the outer part of her moist crevasse, she aimed it at its entrance and then, thrusting her hips forward, pushed me inside.

The woman gave out a deep, guttural groan of pleasure and, after placing her strong, peasant's hands on the sides of my head, captured my lips again with hers and thrust her hungry tongue deep into my mouth.

I had to strain to prevent myself from an immediate explosion of my lusts. I didn't want to deny the impassioned woman the benefit of riding my hardened tool. She was in no hurry to bring me to climax. She moved her hips slowly and gracefully. I could feel her pussy's muscles tightening against me and caressing my rod as if she was equipped with a second mouth down below. It was surprising to find such a practiced whore here so far from civilization. I thought of the fact that I had come thousands of miles, from a place that she could not have imagined in her wildest dreams, from a culture that would stupefy her at its complexity and strangeness and yet our bodies married together naturally. I guess people are the same all over, driven by the same basic needs and desires. It was stupid of me to believe that the woman would not have the same yearnings and bodily needs as any healthy, vibrant, young woman from my own culture. She had a pussy and she had learned how to use it.

I waited until I could hear her give out a little squeal each time that she ascended and descended my pole. Her hips were moving more quickly now and the writhing of her tongue in my mouth had become more energetic and demanding. My hands were gripping her hips like I was holding on to dear life. She gave out an almost mournful moan and I could feel her sex tighten on mine and her body shudder. Her grip on my head tightened and her body pressed forcefully down on mine. I felt my cock explode and its throbbing sent me into convulsions of ecstasy. I jetted my come deep inside her until I felt my loins empty.

My mind was numb as I lay there, the gently sighing, satisfied woman atop me. The old man and his middle wife were still at it and I could hear what could only be Natanya's moans of pleasure nearby. I imagined the virginal young girl's lips between her thighs and my desire for her flesh renewed itself. My cock had softened, but Fio's agile pussy muscles still held it fast within her. Her lips were teasing the flesh of my neck and shoulders and her hands were caressing my arms. I reached my hands up from her hips and took hold of her twin orbs and began to massage them as my lust began to renew.

When my cock had reached hardness again, I turned the lusty Asian woman to her back and took control of our lovemaking. I thrust my hips against hers feverishly as she cried and moaned. She came twice while I was plowing her, screaming her pleasure loudly in the small hut. This time, when I came, I fell against her exhausted.

CHAPTER EIGHT

In the morning, I was alone in the hut when I awoke. Our gear had been brought into the small, round structure and a pile of clothes lay next to my blanket. The fire was going strongly in the middle of the room. I looked quickly around the room for the black valise containing the gold and I saw it lodged against the wall not far from me. I rose and dressed quickly. Natanya had arranged for a pair of heavy, black, corduroy pants, a t-shirt and a heavy, woolen sweater. There was also a brand new pair of high topped leather work boots with thick, leather soles. I was tying off one of the boots when Fio entered. She was dressed as the day before and she gave me a shy, appreciative smile.

The pot on the fire contained a thick porridge and she spooned me out an ample bowlful. I ate the gruelish mixture gratefully and washed it down with goat's milk. Fio came over to me and handed me a small, silver cup and then poured a thick, white mixture into it from a narrow, ceramic jug. It smelled sweet and I tossed it back. It was creamy and rich, almost like liquid butter. I had her pour me a second cup and this time savored it slowly. I wondered what it was.

When my belly was full, I decided to go outside to see what was going on. The day was almost painfully bright and the air was crisp and cold. There was a shroud of clouds over the nearby mountains, the storm that Natanya had referred to the day before. The body of the Pakistani was gone, probably dragged off to its lonely, final resting place by the women when they arose this morning. The spider woman and her charge were sitting not far from the hut. They were attired similarly to me and I was disappointed to see Celine's delicate frame covered in the bulky clothes. They were atop a small, stone wall that ran in a semi circle around what looked like a fireplace. Natanya had her arm around Celine's shoulders and she was stroking her hair with her other hand lovingly. It was the first real act of tenderness that the woman had shown the girl since I had met them. I wondered if there was a real, feeling woman underneath the cold, hard exterior of the spider woman after all.

"Good morning, Harry," Natanya greeted me. When she saw me, her body shifted away from her charge and her stroking of her hair came to a stop. It was as if she didn't want to be seen exhibiting any human feeling for the poor, Hungarian girl.

"How was your fuck?" the black haired woman said gaily. "I heard you grunting and groaning and Fio didn't sound like she was disappointed either."

"Very satisfying, Natanya," I returned. "But when I heard you groaning with lust next to us, I had the urge to come over and give you a taste of my cock."

"That'll be the day, Harry," Natanya replied.

"So what are we supposed to do here all day?" I asked her.

"Just relax and enjoy the view, Harry," Natanya answered. "Take a walk, get some exercise. You should get acclimated to the thinner air up here anyway. It'll be a lot thinner where we're going."

I looked around the fields surrounding the clump of Stone Age buildings and decided that Natanya had a good idea. The goats were out of their corral and were feeding on the scruffs of grass that covered the rolling landscape. A boy, about twelve or thirteen years old had appeared out of nowhere and was tending them, a six foot long pole in his hand. There were three sturdy, short horses in the field with them. I realized that they were some of the pack animals that Natanya had mentioned, but I wondered where the rest of them were. Did the old Chinese man expect us to walk up the mountain for three days to the monastery? If so, I decided that Natanya's suggestion was a good one.

I took a deep breath of air and began to walk up the hill away from the huts. I discovered the truth in Natanya's comment about the air and my chest felt only half filled. I must have walked about five or six miles before I got back to the huts. The scenery was more than beautiful as I strolled, breaking in my new boots and getting my lungs used to the thin air. The vista of the towering mountains was awe inspiring. On the other side, once I crested the hill that stood behind the huts, I could see far into the valley below. What is it about unspoiled nature that brings out our wistful natures? All kinds of thoughts ran through my mind as I walked. My life had been so full of tension and fear over the past many months. And before that, there had been the hard, cold, stone walls of the joint. My life in Atlantic City as Tony's bad boy seemed empty and shallow. What kind of life did I really want? Could I find a little corner of the world, surrounded by natural beauty like this and be satisfied with just living? We all have fantasies of retiring to some simple patch of land somewhere and abandoning the entanglements of society. How simple and pleasurable life could be if we could shed our desires for wealth and status and just live. But it was a fantasy, I knew that. And by the time that I returned to the huts, my thighs aching from their exertions, my lungs burning, I had returned to what I was.

Natanya and Celine had apparently gone on a walk of their own. Kien was sitting on the stone wall smoking his pipe as if expecting someone. I sat down near him and one of the women came over and gave me a bowl filled with strips of dried meat and a wooden cup filled with warm goat's milk. I sat there restoring my energy while the old, Chinese man sat there silently, his eyes seemingly scanning the horizon every once in a while.

I had eaten my lunch and was about to get up and stretch my legs again when I saw what Kien had been waiting for. He had spotted it long before me. There was a trio of sturdy, long maned horses coming up the hill. A man sat on the first one wearing the same kind of sheepskin vest and hat that Kien was wearing. As he neared, I saw that the two other horses were piled high with bundles and that the last one towed a large box of some kind covered with a tarp and sliding along behind it on a travois, two long poles formed into a 'v', the narrow end by the rear of the horse, the wide end dragging along the ground. It bumped and swayed as it was dragged along, Indian style.

Kien didn't react until the man was just upon us. The man on the small horse was younger and slimmer than Kien, but had the same weathered face and fierce looking eyes. The man descended from his perch on the lead horse and came over to where we were sitting. Kien stood and called out a gruff greeting and the men shook hands. Kien nodded to me and uttered some kind of explanation for my presence. The new man nodded to me and took a seat on the wall. I apparently did not warrant a handshake.

The women had emerged from wherever they had been and whatever they had been doing and took hold of the reins of the horses and led them to the flat area in front of the semi-circle of stones. Fio rushed into the hut and returned with another bowl of meat and one of the goatskins filled with the potent liquor.

We three men sat on the stone wall for about an hour drinking Kien's booze. The two Chinese men talked and laughed with each other. They were in no hurry to complete whatever business they had in mind. Finally, the two men stood and began to address the bundles on the horses. Kien did not look at them and had the women carry them over to one of the small huts. As the women took the bundles of presumed contraband away, the men went to the rear of the last horse and untied the tarp covering the large box.

I was surprised to see that it wasn't a box at all. It was a bamboo cage lashed together with primitive rope. Inside the cage was the real surprise. It was a woman. She was young and pretty, with long, black hair. Her hands were tied to the front of the cage, peeking through the bars, and her feet were tied off behind her, the soles extending outside of the bamboo cage. She was crouched down on her knees and a thick wedge of leather had been tied across her mouth pulling her lips back grotesquely. She was naked and her skin was dirty and muddy. Her bare breasts dangled below her chest as she knelt down in the small enclosure. She was obviously Chinese, but she looked different than Kien and the others. Her face and eyes was rounder and her build, although sturdy, was shorter. She squinted at the sudden intrusion of light into her little world and then turned her head towards me. Her face was a model of apprehension and fear.

The men unlashed the cage from the travois and carried it to the middle of the semi-circular, stone wall. After placing it on the ground, they both stood back to admire its feminine contents. The girl whined as she sensed the men appraising her. Her head jerked back and forth, taking in her primitive surroundings. The stranger untied her hands and feet from the cage and then unfastened the ties that held the rear portion of it to the top and swung it down. He grabbed the frightened young woman by the foot and dragged her out.

The girl stood there docilely, tears flowing down her face as Kien examined her. He put his hands on her broad shoulders and assessed their strength. He ran his hands over her round hips and then pinched and prodded her thighs. He reached behind her head, untied the cruel gag that held her lips distended, and then, pinching the sides of her face with his large, wrinkled hand, looked at her teeth. When he was done, he sat back down on the wall while the other man tied the girl's hands off behind her back and then shoved her to the ground.

The men argued and gesticulated for the next half hour or so. Every once and a while one of them would rise from the wall to manhandle the girl as if pointing out some feature of her. The stranger grabbed her by the hair and brought her to her knees and then caressed and stroked one of her breasts. He put his lips on her thick, fat teat and sucked on it noisily until it was hard and stiff. He then turned to Kien and, squeezing the breast firmly until the girl gave a squeal, made his point. Kien knelt down next to the man and pushed the girl over so that her face was in the dirt. He rudely thrust her thighs apart and placed his hand between them seizing her hairy, black bush. He stroked and prodded her quim until it was moist and distended. When his hand was covered with her moisture, he removed it and took a knowledgeable whiff of his fingers. Giving a little grunt of approval, he resumed his seat on the wall.

We drank some more of Kien's brew and then the men, having apparently reached agreement, exchanged a small wad of currency. Kien's women had brought some new bundles from the storage hut and the men tied them off on the horses. Kien and the stranger shook hands and the man hopped up on his horse while the women tied off ropes leading from the bridles of the two other horses to the tails of the ones in front. The stranger gave a shout of goodbye, circled the horses and trod off the way he had come.

The girl gave out a little cry when she saw that the stranger was leaving her here. The import of the last hour or so was clear: she had been sold. I wondered how the other women were going to react to a fourth wife. She was prettier and slimmer than the other women and younger too. Kien arose and, picking the girl's primitive gag up from the dust, tied it off harshly behind her head, silencing her once more.

We sat there a while taking in the forlorn aspect of the Chinese girl. Kien patiently smoked his pipe. Natanya and Celine appeared back from their walk. It had warmed considerably and the women had removed their sweaters. Natanya was wearing a black, silk chemise under hers with thin straps running over her shoulders. Her heavy breasts swayed gently behind it as she walked and I could see her inviting nipples stiffened by the still somewhat brisk air. Celine had apparently not been issued this dainty garment and she was naked from the waist up. Her pretty breasts flounced and swayed as she descended the hill, her small, fragile hand in Natanya's.

"I see that Kien's package has arrived," Natanya said gaily. Her eyes flowed over the girl's flesh, appraising it expertly. Celine's eyes were wide with astonishment. She nervously tried to hold back as the older woman drew her closer. "Isn't she pretty, Celine?"

Celine just held her lips tightly together. All of Natanya's questions to her where rhetorical. The girl's continual silence, broken only by her moans and grunts of passion when she came, made her seem more fragile and enticing than she would have been anyway.

Natanya spoke to Kien and the man shrugged his shoulders and gave a grunt. He shouted out a command to his wives and two of them lifted the Chinese girl from her knees and started to escort her over to the barn.

"What's going on," I asked Natanya.

"I told you that Kien's people had been pushed out of their homes by the Han Chinese. He and his friends are conducting a low level guerilla war against them. This girl is Han. She was probably taken on a raid."

"So what are they going to do to her?" I asked.

"Why don't you go and see, Harry? I'll bet you'll enjoy it."

Kien had gotten to his feet and was waiting for me to join him. I decided that this was something that I did not want to miss and I walked off with him towards the barn. From the corner of my eye I saw Fio bring Celine and Natanya their lunch.

The barn door had been left open and when I stepped inside I saw that Kien's wives had the Chinese girl on her knees in the middle of it. The floor was of well packed earth. There were eight small stalls around the perimeter, their interiors closed off from view by swinging doors that went down almost to the floor. The doors were affixed closed with leather knots.

The women forced the struggling, crying Chinese girl forward until they had her neck imprisoned in a long, wooden yoke that was mounted in front of her. When they untied the girl's gag from behind her head, I heard her dismayed voice crying out for the first time. Her voice was high pitched and frantic as she yelled out a string of musical Chinese words. She was obviously pleading for mercy and was terrified as to what these cruel women had in mind for her.

The older woman got up and went over to a cabinet by the wall and returned with a small pair of shears and a razor. The other woman, Kien's middle wife, had produced a large, leather ball with a small lead protruding from it. She grabbed the Chinese girl by her hair and lifted her face up, exposing her mouth. The unhappy, naked, young girl was in the middle of a plea when Kien's wife shoved the large ball into her mouth. It was somewhat larger than the opening and the young girl's lips had to stretch painfully to accommodate it. But, after a moment, it plopped right in and the girl's desperate entreaties were reduced to a murmur.

While the young girl cried, wife number one immediately went to work. She took long sheaves of the Chinese girl's jet black hair and sliced them off. She worked along the sides of the girl's head until the smooth, shiny black hair was reduced to stubble. She then scissored the hair down the middle of the girl's head until all that was left was a short, two inch wide Mohican. She left the hairs at the back of the girl's head intact so that it looked like she had a long, black tail emanating from the back of her neck.

Suddenly, I had a terrible insight as to what was happening to the girl. Natanya had used the term 'pack animals', not horses. The stalls were too small for horses anyway. I had heard feint whimpers and what sounded like whinnies coming from the stalls as the Chinese girl was having her hair shorn but had paid it no mind. I stepped over to the nearest stall and, releasing the tie that held the door closed, pulled it open.

There, kneeling in a pile of dirty straw, was a woman, or what once had been a woman. Her mouth was confined by the same type of large, leather ball that had been used to silence the Chinese girl. Her face and eyes were similar to the young girl who Kien had just bought. There was a thick, brass ring through her nose that was connected by a leather strap to a ring in the wall in the rear of her stall about five feet above the floor. A strip of two inch long, coal black hair ran down the middle of her otherwise bald head terminating in a tightly braided pony tail that reached down to her waist. Her arms were confined behind her. She gave me a doleful, passive look that bespoke her resignation to her fate and readiness to endure whatever I had in mind for her.

'Pack animals,' Natanya had said! The girl was a pack animal! I had heard of such things but had put the concept off as some strange, perverse fantasy. Some of the men at the resort liked to hook the slave girls up to carts and make them haul them around the golf course, but that's about as far as that went. This was the real thing. The beast woman in the stall seemed maybe between 25 or thirty years old. It was hard to tell due to the bizarre grimace on her face. When I looked closely at her mouth, I could see that it was formed into a narrow circle, just about the circumference of a rampant cock, and that there were leather stitches around her distended lips. Her eyebrows had been shaven off, which, taken together with her gruesome, round smile, deprived her visage of almost all aspects of humanity. Her thighs were spread widely and I could see that her hairless sex had been stitched up by a thick, leather lacework. Her breasts and belly carried faint scars reminiscent of abuse by a whip, but were unmarred by any cruel adornments. Little bells had been affixed to rings that went through her ears.

Kien stepped next to me and clapped his hand on my shoulder. When I looked at him I could see his proud visage. A man proud of his stock. I shuddered at his cruelty.

And that of his women. For they clearly cooperated and facilitated these creature's cruel fates. I wondered how many were there.

Kien took me around the barn and opened each door for my examination of the rest of his herd. A couple of the stalls held two women. They all stared back at me forlornly when he opened the doors to their stalls and then fearfully at their owner. But it was the last stall that was apparently Kien's pride and joy. He opened its door with a flourish. There, standing on either side of the stall, their necks confined by yokes built into the walls, were two unhappy creatures in foal. Their bellies protruded from their torsos in wide arcs. Their feet were tied apart and fastened to the floor. Their breasts were large and full, almost bursting. Kien stepped up closer to one of them and, seizing one of her bulging breasts with one hand, caressed and squeezed it. After a moment, a dollop of milk appeared at her nipple. He leaned over and took a long suckle at her teat. The girl gave out a sigh and her knees weakened.

So this was what Fio had given me to drink this morning. I was appalled at how much I had enjoyed it. It was like finding out that you were a cannibal.

Kien stepped back and invited me to have a suckle. I remembered his knife and how handily he wielded it and I gave him a polite smile. I looked into the Chinese girl's doleful eyes for a moment and then lowered my head to her breast. When I sucked at her teat, a hot, sweet, creamy liquid poured into my mouth. I confess to say that it was delicious. My cock stiffened at the warmth of her fat, full breast in my hand and the nakedness of her body. As I enticed her milk from her tit, the girl moaned and her body shuddered. Her pussy had been untied and I dropped my hand to it. It was widely dilated and wet. I caressed it, encouraging the girl's forced enjoyment of her ordeal.

I could hear the girl outside the stall squealing and protesting and I decided to go back and witness the rest of her conversion to a beast of burden. The sides of her head had now been shaven clean and Kien's middle wife was smearing some kind of ointment over the bare skin of her cranium. Wife no. 1 was behind the girl and, having untied her wrists, was retying them. She had matched her left wrist to the crook of her right arm and was bringing the other hand to a similar position with her left arm. There was what looked like wide, leather straps soaking in a murky, thick liquid in a pail. When the wrists were securely bound, she began to wrap the straps around the flattened, parallel, lower portions of her arms.

Working carefully from one wrist to the other, she wound the straps tightly, smoothing them out as they adhered to her skin. The girl was crying and struggling but she had little chance of dissuading the strong, sturdy, peasant woman from her task. The girl's hands had been pressed against her elbows palm up and when Kien's wife put on the second coat of long, thin, wide straps, she carefully covered the girl's fingers and hands, cementing them in place. When wife no. 1 was done, she stood and carried the pail away. I looked down at the Chinese girl's bound arms and hands and realized that they would probably be denied to her for the rest of her short, miserable life. I could see the thick, syrupy substance that covered the straps hardening even as I watched it.

They were not yet done with the girl. Wife no. 2 had brought over a hollow, wooden block that was cut in half and reattached with hinges on one side. She released the Chinese girl's head from the yoke and pushed her back on her knees. The older wife held the girl's head still while the wooden block was affixed around her neck. It banged shut ominously and the women locked it closed. The girl's frantic face shook and contorted in her confinement. The block was tall enough so that it rested on her collarbone and the other end pushed her chin up high. She had no idea what was coming, but I did. I watched as wife no. 1 produced a round circle of wood covered with leather. It had little tabs sticking out of the bottom and top on one side. Once the lips were spread wide, the tabs would fit over the teeth and lock the jaws apart. The girl's mouth would remain permanently open for as long as she lived.

The middle wife held the girl's head still while the older woman knelt in front of her and presented the infernal device to her mouth. She pulled the short leather string that was attached to the ball in her mouth and pried it out. Tears were flowing down the girl's face and she began to shout and plead piteously once her mouth was emptied. Grabbing her jaw in one of her powerful hands, wife no. 1 squeezed the girl's face harshly. The girl moaned and tried to pull her head away to no avail. The older woman pressed the top edge of the ring gag to her mouth and pushed it cruelly inside her top lip. She held it in place with one hand while wife no. 2 held the girl's head still. Kien was watching with an amused, satisfied look on his face. It must have been enjoyable for him to see a woman from the race that had stolen his people's lands and killed and dispersed them suffering so. For me, the cruelty was horrifying but yet mesmerizing. My days at Klitzman's Isle had eroded my moral qualms at the cruelties that could be visited on female flesh. I pitied the poor Chinese girl but assuaged my guilt at standing by while her humanity was stolen from her by the thought that my presence added nothing to the girl's sufferings. If Klitzman had not sent me on this mysterious quest, I would not have been here and the girl would be suffering just as she was anyway.

But my cock recorded the fact that the sight of her suffering, her nakedness and helplessness was enflaming to my passions. Kien's middle wife glanced up at me while she struggled to keep the Chinese girl's head still. She had a knowing, sly look on her face as if she was aware of the lusts that the cruel tableau was generating in me. Her heavy breasts shook under her dirty, white shift. In spite of myself I wondered what it would be like to affix my lips to them. Maybe I would find out.

It was the moment of crises for the young Chinese girl. Wife no. 1 had a thick, gleaming, steel needle in her hand. Attached to it was a long, thin strand of leather. The girl screamed as the needle was pushed through her upper lip. The leather thread was pulled through the hole made by the needle until the knot on its end was lodged between her gums and her teeth. Garbled words, indecipherable to me, came from her mouth. Soon she would lose the ability to speak entirely.

Wrapping the thread around the leather encased hoop, wife no. 1 pulled it tight so that the top of the gag was forced up into the space between the girl's upper lip and her gums. The older woman pressed the loop forward until the tab on the top clicked across and behind the top of the girl's teeth, capturing them. She quickly drew another stitch and then another while the girl howled. She worked her way counterclockwise, marrying the girl's lips to the hoop. When she reached the bottom, she carefully fit the bottom of the ring inside the girl's lip while making sure that the bottom tab covered the girl's gleaming, white, lower teeth. She then, remorselessly ignoring the formerly pretty girl's cries and wails, continued up the other side. When she reached the top, she cut the leather thread and then tied it off inside the girl's now circular oral opening.

Blood from the Chinese girl's wound trickled down from her mouth. She was moaning inconsolably. Wife no. 1 sat back and admired her work. She took the ball of leather and reinserted into the girl's mouth, squeezing it past the leather covered, wooden ring that now distended it. The girl's moans increased from the pain but the sound of them was reduced to a kind of hum. Her eyes looked around the dim barn frantically as if seeking a savior. She was clearly astonished at the cruelty of the strange people who possessed her. I had to admit that it astonished me too. But as much, I was sure, that the girl hoped that her torments were over, I had seen the other women-beasts in their stalls and knew that it was not.

Wife No. 1 gleefully rubbed the miserable and frightened girl on her head, stroking the two inch wide of short black hair that she had left there. She still had the razor by her side and a pail of soapy water with a brush in it. She took the brush and worked up a lather in the bowl and then applied the lather to the girl's bushy, black eyebrows. While wife no. 2 held the girl's head still, wife no. 1 quickly sliced off the arching line of hair above each eye. Soap had spilled down into the girl's eyes and she screeched as she helplessly blinked them in an attempt to relieve her suffering. The women just laughed.

On the floor next to wife no. 1 was a small box and what looked like an awl. She picked up the sharp, pointed tool and, holding onto the girl's ear lobes, punched a hole in each one. The girl screamed again and struggled to free herself from her bonds, but the middle wife held her fast. Wife no. 1 opened the little box and removed two golden ear rings with little bells attached. She fastened the ear rings through the holes she had made and clamped them closed. The girl's shaking and futile movements now produced a pleasant tingling noise. The older woman flicked them with her fingers playfully, laughing at the tinny, melodic sound that they made.

The unhappy Chinese girl looked wholly different than she had less than an hour ago. Her distorted face, her shorn locks, the absence of the humanizing growth above her eyes made her seem like some strange creature. Kien had been watching impassively as his wives reduced the girl to a beast-like visage. He barked some order to his wives and wife no. 1 nodded agreeably and ran to get a wide, three legged stool from the other side of the barn. She placed it down in front of the Chinese girl and then she and the second wife lifted the girl up and draped her across it. Her ankles had been tied with short leads that ran to rings in the floor and her thighs were spread open. I could see her pouting nether lips covered with her thick thatch of stark, black, pubic hair. Kien loosened his trousers and knelt behind the prone, former woman.

When the Chinese girl felt the man's hand on her loins, her muffled protests began anew. The women held her torso down firmly on the stool as Kien explored her cleft with his large, bony hand. She was helpless to resist the expert digits that explored her defenseless quim and soon I could see a telltale glistening between her nether lips. When satisfied at her readiness, Kien aimed his hardened cock at the girl's plush entrance and slid himself in. He paused momentarily, apparently encountering evidence of the girl's virginity. He drew his hips back a few inches and pushed forwards again, harder this time. The girl gave out a cry of pain and dismay at her deflowerment. Kien paid her squeals no mind as he began to stroke himself easily and steadily inside her now womanly canal.

It was exciting to watch the old man at work on the helpless female's body. His rigid pole ran easily in and out of her puss as she cried and moaned at her violation. Kien's head was tilted back and his oval, deep black eyes were squinting, almost closed, as he enjoyed the girl's fecund hole. His wives looked on with admiration and not without some jealousy as their man took his pleasure within the new pack animal. The middle wife, who had a curvaceous body of her own, kept looking at me with a lascivious grin. I deduced from her constant attentions to me that she would indeed be my bed companion tonight.

I could see that the aged Asian was nearing his point of completion. His face was strained and his thrusts into the back of the pinioned girl's thighs had become more insistent. Suddenly he pulled his long, thick cock from the girl's sopping crevasse and, taking the blood stained instrument in his hand, aimed at the dainty star between her plump rear cheeks. The girl's squealing became more intense, muffled, of course, by the sound deadening leather ball in her mouth, as Kien pressed his cock home. He had his hands on her delicious globes, their halves parted with his large, gnarly hands. I watched the end of his tool pass through the little ring and the girl screamed in pain. Her thighs and ankles were twitching and shuddering and her torso was twisting on the stool on which she was held prisoner. As I watched her posterior being violated, I gave my stiffened cock a little rub underneath my thick, corduroy pants.

The sheepskin clad Asian man gave out a loud grunt of satisfaction and his grip tightened on the girl's ass as he came. The Chinese girl's screams had reduced to sobs as she received her new master's spunk. I was sure that it was the first of many times that she would feel the man's rod dumping his essence deep within her. Who could resist the ready availability of her flesh despite her now subhuman status? She might learn to eventually look forward to her use by her cruel owner as a break in what I was sure was the monotonous routine of life in the small, dark barn. Some day, I was sure, she would be standing where the other two beast women were standing now, her belly protruding, her breasts giving off the sweet, thick cream that the Asians who had broken her treated as a refined delicacy.

Kien took a moment to enjoy the after effects of his discharge and then slowly withdrew his weapon from the girl's bowels. Wife no. 2 was ready with a bowl of soapy water and a cloth and she dutifully cleaned the girl's wastes and the evidence of her deflowerment from her husband's cock, stroking it and caressing it lovingly. Kien nodded to me and gave a wave towards the supine female. I understood him to indicate that it was my turn to plow the furrows that he had opened. I don't excuse it, but I hope you understand the compulsion created by the combination of my passion, the delectable, vibrant young body of the unfortunate Chinese girl and the spirit of encouragement that I received from Kien and his wives. Not to mention the loss of face that I feared from the knife wielding Asian. I was to spend the better part of the next week with him on our trek to the monastery deep in the Hindu Kush and back and I didn't want to have to worry about whether he had doubts as to my character as a tough, ruthless motherfucker. Besides, when in Rome. You know what I mean?

I fished my hardened cock from my pants and knelt down behind the now quietly sobbing girl. As soon as she realized that there was another male behind her intent on ravishment, she gave a low, disconsolate moan. But she did not struggle during my assault. Her pussy was still lush and distended from her prior fucking and, despite the tightness of this aperture, my needy cock slid right in. Her hot, sweaty flesh trembled beneath my fingertips as I spread my hands over her soft rear cheeks and over her naked back.

The bells on her ears tingled pleasantly as her body jerked at each of my hard thrusts. My rod was soon infused with my impending orgasm and, like my predecessor in perversion, I slipped it from the girl's hot cunt and plunged it in her still gaping anal passage. She gave out a piteous wail as she felt my cock penetrate her most private place. The ring of her sphincter was tight along the shaft of my cock as I rasped it back and forth within her. I felt my cock begin to spurt and jerk and the pleasure of my climax made my body shiver. My mind pushed out all qualms over my participation in the girl's degradation and welcomed happily the waves of ecstasy that my loins were sending it.

When my cock's convulsions were done, I withdrew my spent meat from the girl's body. Kien's second wife happily washed my tool. I detected a particular relish in her of the heft of my manhood and she tugged and caressed it just a moment or so longer than necessary purely for hygienic purposes. Although the woman was middle aged, certainly over 40, she retained some of the vigor of her youth in her face. Her touch was remarkably soft and knowing as she handled my meat and she gave off an earthy, pungent, but not unpleasant smell as she knelt before me. To those of you who disdain mature women, I must respectfully demure. The hard and tensile flesh of young beauties is something to be enjoyed together with their vigor and their exuberant enjoyment of the pleasures of their bodies. But the flesh of the mature woman is to be savored, like a fine cognac, sipped at and appreciated for its laconic delight and the exquisite blend of flavors that her prior experiences have brought her. The Asian man's middle wife was like that and I immediately began to anticipate our upcoming evening sojourn.

Kien and I stood by and watched as the women completed their work on the girl. After they had turned the limp girl to her back and spread her thighs in a yoke, wife no. 1 quickly scraped away the black morass of hair that surrounded her insulted sexual slit. The girl cried and moaned, her eyes transmitting her forlornness as the old woman sewed her now smooth and hairless love lips together. The girl strained at the bindings that held her thighs widely ajar. There would be no unwanted pregnancies in Kien's herd. Two beasts in foal at a time presumably satisfied their wants for the delicious product of their breasts. The top of the girl's pussy was left open, just enough to slide a little finger in and her pleasure bud was left exposed. Wife no 1 made sure of this by giving the small button a series of caresses with one of her misshapen, wrinkled fingers. She waited to see the nascent signs of unwanted passion on the girl's animal like face before she brought her ministrations to a halt. Afterwards, the old woman cleaned the stitched together love lips of the blood that had seeped from the piercings of the steel needle.

Meanwhile, wife no 2. had stoked up a fire in the small, cast iron stove that heated the chilly, damp barn. I could see a long, iron handle protruding from it.

The girl was brought back to her knees and wife no 1 introduced a large, pincer like device to the young girl's nasal cavity. Her face contorted and she moaned as the old woman punched a large hole in her septum. Blood poured from the girl's nose. The older woman soon staunched the flow with a small iron bar that she retrieved from the fire. The Chinese girl howled with pain as the woman sealed off the torn flesh within her nose. Kien's middle wife brought a large, shiny brass ring from the cabinet by the wall. It had a gap in it so that one of its ends could be poked through the hole that had been made in the girl's nasal divide. The women forced the girl's head down on the stool that she had lain on a short while before and, after removing the wooden block that had confined her neck, turned her head sideways. Madam Kien, Sr., banged the brilliant, gold colored ornament on its side with a small, ball peen hammer until the ring was made whole and the gap between the ends closed. The ring gave a little 'click' as it married together.

The girl was now equipped with the accouterments of her new life. The large, golden ring in her nose would be useful in confining her to a tree or a post and the little bells would announce her presence where ever she roamed. If she tried to run away, the sound of the tinkling, brass bells would betray her to anyone following. Her hands, which might have found a way to undo the locks on the barn, fought off the ministrations and/or cruelties of her master or her mistresses, were permanently bound behind her. And her mouth was readily available for feeding and liquid refreshment or the insertion of a cock in need.

The women brought the girl to a standing position. Her limp body sagged in their arms. I don't believe that the girl was aware of the nefarious instrument heating in the stove.

The women attached a harness around the girl's chest. It had rings above the shoulders and the women tied long, leather straps around them and the tossed the free ends over a rafter. They pulled the unfortunate, former young woman to the tips of her toes and tied the straps off to the rings on her shoulders. The harness left the girl's delectable, swaying breasts fully exposed.

Kien took down a long, evil looking lash from the wall. He unfurled it casually in front of the girl. Her eyes widened and the energy returned to her body when she saw what it was. I knew from my experiences at Klitzman's Isle that it was best that a slave girl learn as soon as possible the consequences of disobedience. Most of our pretty, new female guests danced at the end of whip for the first time in their sheltered lives within hours of their arrival. The new horse woman would now be indoctrinated into what would happen should she be less than enthusiastic in her soon to come training on how to best serve her master as an unquestioning, obedient, abject beast of burden.

Kien let the whip rip. The girl's body stiffened and she gave a howl that filled the small structure with its piteous sound, echoing off of the stone walls and reverberating on the wooden constructs that served as the horse-women's stalls. A long, fiery, red welt rose immediately across the girl's pretty breasts. Her legs danced and hopped in place as her harness kept her centered in the room. Her body turned due to her frantic movements, exposing her plump, enticing rear. The cruel Asian laid the whip across her defenseless derriere and the girl's howling accelerated in volume. I was surprised that she could make that loud a noise with the gag in her mouth, but she did. The intense, maroon line that formed across her buttocks was divided by the cleft of her ass.

The poor girl suffered five strokes of the fierce whip before Kien brought her ordeal to a halt. After all, she was not really being punished. She was just being given a little bit of encouragement. She would remember her first whipping for a long, long time. Whipping her now, while she was eminently impressionable, might save her the experience of it later. It would certainly serve as motivation to do her best while she was trained to lope along with a heavy pack on her back.

I would guess that the formerly attractive, young girl was thinking that there was not much more that her cruel captors could do to her. If she did, she was wrong. Kien walked over to the stove and, after putting some heavy, insulated gloves on his hands, pulled out the iron bar that had been heating there. Its end was a bright red. It terminated in a square plate with some kind of oriental ideogram on it. The ideogram was set out from the plate a good quarter inch.

The women quickly undid the straps that had held the Chinese girl's body in place and deftly dragged her limp body across the barn to a waist high, wooden stanchion. They draped the girl's body over it and, while one affixed a strap to her nose ring and connected it to a ring in the floor, the other bound her ankles together and affixed them to a ring on the other side. A strap went around the poor girl's waist, fastening her torso in place and making still and available her plump, pale ass and also above and below her knees, ensuring that her legs were properly confined. They spread some straw around her feet.

The girl's body struggled in her bindings while wife no. 1 took the soapy cloth and washed off a portion of her right rump. Kien had put the iron back in the fire so that the end would remain ready for use. He retrieved it when he saw that the young girl was properly secured and prepared for her disfigurement. He stepped forward quickly and, after pausing to take careful aim, pressed the glowing red end of the branding iron against the young woman's skin. There was a sharp hissing sound followed by a bellowing scream from the young girl. The smell of burnt flesh immediately suffused throughout the small structure. Kien held the 4" by 4" square to the girl's flesh while it burned away her flesh, indelibly marking it with his sign. The girl lost control of herself in her agony and piss and shit flowed from her orifices down her thick thighs to the floor. And then, mercifully, she passed out.

When Kien removed he branding iron, there was a deep, angry, red scar on the girl's rear. The iron had burnt a square into her flesh. Inside the square, burned ¼" deeper was the strange, primitive looking form of the red hot ideogram. Later, Natanya told me that the ideogram marked each horse woman as, 'Beast of Kien'.

CHAPTER NINE

We left the exhausted, forlorn girl where she was to recover from her ordeal. Kien barked an imperative to his number one wife and she nodded. She went over to the stall holding the pregnant women-beasts and opened the stall door. I stood by while she tested the belly and sex of the woman to the right. As Kien's wife's knowledgeable hands pushed and massaged her belly, I noticed that it was lower then the belly of the woman standing affixed to the other side of the small stall. Her belly had dropped, indicating the relative immanency of the birth of her child. I wondered who the father was. Did Kien use the beast women as a harem to breed his own children? I didn't think so and, other than the boy I had seen earlier, who seemed to disappear as mysteriously as he appeared, there were no children about.

I was told later by Natanya that the tribe had a male Han Chinese man captive. He was a former wrestler and then a soldier in the Chinese People's Army. He had been taken of one of their raids. Deprived of sight and hearing, his tongue cut out, he was brought around the various outposts from time to time to cover the beast women in heat who had been chosen to breed. The man practically senseless from his confinement and various tortures, but he was aware enough so that when he was placed in a cage with one of the beast women he knew what to do. He would be kept in a cage with the woman or women until they had shown signs of conception and then be moved on. Kien generally refrained from fucking the beast women in their pussies and only did so once he knew that they couldn't conceive due to being already pregnant. Kien's own children, bred off of his three wives, were being raised in a remote village thought to be safe from the reach of the punishing hand of the Chinese government and away from the 'corruptions' of the equally despised Pakistanis.

Wife number one pressed her hand into the bound and disconcerted woman's sexual pouch and spoke some words in her guttural language to Kien. Kien gave a grunt and what I assumed to be an instruction. In obedience to her husband's direction, the old woman left the stall and came back with a wicker basket. The basket was lined with a thick, soft, woolen blanket. She placed the basket between the horse woman's legs and then, unfastening her neck from the yoke that held her standing upright, put her hands on the pregnant woman's shoulders and forced her into a crouch. There were pegs on the wall just below the naked former human female's head and the old woman refastened the yoke around her neck and connected it to the wall. She tied off the pregnant woman's thighs so that they were spread widely and then put a brown, leather, sheepskin hood over her head.

Apparently, the beast woman was expected to birth directly into the basket below her. The hood would prevent her from seeing her spawn and forming any attachment to it. I speculated that the child that would be produced would be considered of little value or they would have taken greater precautions for its safety. But Natanya later assured me that the practice had been used for many years and that they rarely lost one. After all, the beast women were in excellent physical shape and, being well fed and well exercised, usually produced healthy and hearty offspring. Those that failed to survive the lack of immediate care after their birth would probably not have survived anyway.

As a last measure to ensure the quick and easy delivery, the old woman began to stroke the pregnant woman's distended cleft. It did not take long before the crouching woman was giving out her distorted moans of pleasure from behind her coarse, leather hood. Her moisture was gushing from her dilated cleft and I could see her thighs trembling in her passion. Her full breasts heaved and shook as her breaths became deeper and deeper. The lust driven woman, much to the old woman's and Kien's amusement, started to grunt and moan as she came. I could see her toes curl under her feet and her body shudder as her orgasm overcame her. Her belly shook and the sides of her distended stomach contracted with each spasm of her womb. When her cries subsided, the old woman withdrew her moisture covered hand and wiped it on the beast woman's chest.

Outside the barn, it was still daylight and it took me a moment to adjust my eyes to its brightness. The sun was about halfway down the sky to the southwest. I was astounded by my experience. I don't think that I will ever forget the forlorn look on the Chinese girl's face as bit by bit her humanity was stripped from her. The idea that human beings in this day and age could keep their fellow creatures in such harsh bondage should not have been a revelation to me. After all, I had come from Klitzman's island where feminine rights were non-existent. It wasn't really such a huge jump from making pretty, young women sexual slaves to turning them into horses. But somehow the concept of denying them every semblance of human dignity seemed beyond the pale.

I strolled back over to the main hut with Kien. Natanya was there, sitting on the rock wall, having a little chat with Fio, Kien's number three wife. Girl talk. I looked around for the pretty Celine and, for a few moments did not see her. Then I looked at the bamboo cage that had been the Chinese girl's prison when she arrived maybe an hour and a half ago.

The pretty, delicate Celine was ensconced inside the cage. Her clothing was outside it and she was kneeling on the slats that served as the cage's floor, naked. Her arms had been drawn behind her and bound together. She had one of the large, leather ball gags in her mouth. She looked just about as disconsolate and unhappy as I had yet seen her. A wave of protest rose within me as I speculated that Natanya had decided to let Kien turn the child like orphan into one of his horse women. I decided then and there that I would not let it happen. My .45 was on my shoulder and I carefully and quietly unfastened the strap that held it securely in the holster. Kien was behind me and I realized that I would have to do him first.

Natanya looked up at me when she finally heard me approach. "Harry," she called out. "Did you learn all about the ponygirls? What do you think? Should we turn Celine into a ponygirl? She'd look so cute prancing around all the time naked with her arms tied behind her."

I stopped a few yards away from Natanya so as to let Kien pass me. I wanted him where I could put a hole in him before he put one in me. "I don't think that I would like that, Natanya," I answered. My voice was colder and harsher than I intended. Kien, surprised by my tone stepped to my side warily.

I could see Celine shivering and quaking in her cage. I didn't know if she was aware of what I had just witnessed, but having been placed in a cage and having seen the Chinese girl ominously hauled away, I was sure she had an idea of what the spider woman was talking about.

Natanya stared at me, her eyes cold and hard. "Listen, Harry, Celine belongs to me. I'll do anything I want with her. Do you understand?"

All of the cruel woman's evil nature crept out in her harsh, venomous statement. There was a long, few moments of tension. My hand wanted to take hold of the handle of my .45, but I didn't want to start in motion another round of death, maybe even my own. My heart beat wildly in my chest and my palms were sweaty. I started to count to five.

Suddenly, as if we were sitting in some Parisian parlor discussing the latest fashions, Natanya broke out into a refined, feminine laughter. "Oh, Harry," she said. "You take things too seriously. I was only joking." She looked at her imprisoned ward and spoke to her. "You knew I was joking, Celine, didn't you? I wouldn't do that to you. You're too pretty and delicate to be a ponygirl."

Celine, of course couldn't reply with her mouth full of the leather ball, and Natanya didn't expect an answer in any case. I let my breath out slowly. Kien's body, which had tensed in expectation of shit breaking out, relaxed.

"Then what is she doing in the cage then?" I asked, trying to hide my relief at not having generated mayhem.

"Oh I think she looks so pretty in there, don't you, Harry? I have a little cage for her at home and she's used to it. It's much nicer of course, but we are roughing it after all. I'll let her out in a while. I'm sure that she'll be appropriately grateful for your concern for her."

My cock, even though recently serviced, gave a little twitch as I thought of the pretty girl's lips around my pole. I was indeed a tarnished hero. I was willing to kill and maybe die to prevent her from being turned into a beast, but was also willing to rape her mouth any time. And do more if he spider woman would let me.

The tension abated, I decided to fish my bottle of gin out of my carry bag and take a strong snort. I went in the hut and retrieved it. I wanted to go for another walk, both to continue to prepare myself for our trek in the morrow and to get away from Natanya's evil gaze and the memories of the women locked in Kien's barn. Holding the bottle by its neck, I stepped out of the hut and started to walk up the hill next to it. I heard Natanya's mocking voice behind me.

"Don't forget to come back and get your blowjob, Harry!"

I walked for about a half an hour until I found a spot I thought suitable to sit and think. I plopped myself down in the sparse grass and took a swig from the gin bottle. It burned good going down. I took another.

From where I sat, I could see the assembly of small, stone huts about a hundred feet below me and a good half a mile away. On my right, I could look down into the vast valley. The sun was beginning to turn the sky pink in preparation of the evening lightshow. It had turned slightly orange and had grown bigger, the effects of the bending of its rays of light by earth's gravity. On my left were the looming Hindu Kush Mountains. Tomorrow I would be scaling them. I wondered what surprises they had in store for me. What of value could a remote Asian monastery hold for Klitzman? Would the spider woman and her ethnic Chinese ally, whose foibles she seemed to know so well, turn on me there? I had a vision of my lifeless body being tossed down some lonely, remote ravine, and shuddered. Well, what did it matter where I died? There was no one to mourn me, except perhaps Carol. But she might right now at this very moment be suffering cruelly at the hands of one of the masters back at Klitzman's island, cursing me for not saving her, lamenting that she had ever put her trust in me. Or she could have been sold off. Maybe she had already been disposed of when I emerged from Klitzman's dungeon. The fat man was the devil himself and wasn't the devil the Prince of Lies? Klitzman had told me what I needed to hear so that I would agree to go on this mystery tour for him. Kill for him. Do anything dastardly that my mission required.

I took another swig of gin and lay back as its soothing burn went through me. I should have bought a couple more bottles when I had the chance. There were only a few inches of the precious, clear liquid left. There was Kien's potent brew, but that was not mine. I didn't like to have to depend on another man's generosity for my booze.

The effects of the booze and my emotional rollercoaster caused me to doze off. My dreams were troubled and disturbing. I don't know how long I napped, but I awoke to the sound of tintillating bells. For a moment, I thought it was still a part of my dreams. When I sat up I saw what it was. The horse women had been released from their barn and were taking an afternoon peramble. They were ascending the hill on which I lay at a steady pace. The bells on their ears recorded each strained step as they hurried their way towards me. They were wearing replicas of the leather harness I had seen on the Chinese girl earlier, although she was not among them. Even Kien and his cruel wives would know that she needed to recover from her ordeal before being put to work.

Strapped to the back of each sturdy, Asian horse woman was a bulging knapsack. Straps fastened it to the rings on the shoulders of their harnesses. The women were travelling along at a steady pace as they climbed the hill. I could see the strained, sub human face of the lead girl as she approached. Her neck was connected to her sisters behind her by a seven or eight foot long length of chain. The women were moving along much faster than I would have been able to do even without a weight on my back. Their breasts swayed and jolted at each harried step. Their thighs were thick and strong. Kien would undoubtedly bulk the new girl up so that she would be able to bear a load and keep up with these well trained beasts.

The women passed about twenty feet away from me and then made a right turn to proceed along the edge of the flat field on which I lay. Their bodies were covered with sweat and I could hear them huffing and puffing as they went by. Their bells were like a little symphony. It was almost pleasant to watch and listen to the women as they hurried to complete their training session. They all gave me a forlorn, supplicative look as they passed. Not me, I thought. It's not me who will save you.

Surprisingly, despite their uniform disfigurements, I could detect a spark of individuality in each one of them as they looked into my eyes and then went along their way. Eight women, individuals, with different lives and stories, but one, uniform fate. How long could they last as a horse woman or 'ponygirl' as Natanya had called them? If they fell and broke their leg, did Kien slit their throats and toss them into whatever dark place that his women had tossed the Pakistani driver that he had killed yesterday? Did eventually the despair over their miserable lives cause them to break down so that not even the threat of worse forms of punishment could motivate them to go one step further? If that happened, did Kien visit upon them, as an example to the others, the most heinous and excruciating form of death that he could devise so as to discourage the others from surrendering to hopelessness? Surely, Kien's little hamlet wasn't so far beyond the reach of Pakistani law that someone couldn't come up here and put an end to his cruelties. We had driven up here for God's sake! Someone high up must have been protecting him, valuing his services as a smuggler or as an annoyance to the Chinese authorities across the mountains.

I watched the women disappear over the far edge of the hill and listened as the sound of their bells faded away. They were conspicuously unsupervised. It would have taken quite an athlete to keep up with them. Anyway, where would they go? Hands bound behind them, chained together, their voices silenced, they couldn't even stop and take a drink of water if they needed to. And then there were the bells that would betray them every step of their way.

I lay back down after taking another pull of gin. I had come to the bottom and I flung the empty bottle away in disgust. It sailed over the edge of the hill and I could hear it crash against the rocks below. I just lay there, not sleeping this time, letting the remaining warmth of the sun run over me and watching the huge, billowing clouds overhead chase each other across the sky, mate, and then break apart again. It was good to be alive. And although I wasn't really free, I was freer than most. And I had a purpose: destroying Klitzman. Whatever it took. That was what Bederson had told me back in Atlanta. Whatever it took. Okay then. Whatever it took.

I was surprised to hear the tell tale sound of the horse women's bells as they climbed the hill for a second time. They had been gone about twenty minutes. Given ten minutes to climb the hill to where I was, that would make a good two hours of running. I watched with amazement as they passed me once again. Their faces were more strained, sweat was pouring off of them in rivulets. Their chests were heaving with their exertions. But their rock hard thighs kept pumping along. I would hate to be kicked by any of them. It would be like getting kicked by a horse.

After I watched them disappear, I arose from my restful interlude. I would have to face Natanya again, the enticing and frustrating allure of her charge, Celine, and the fearful knife of the cruel Kien. But it was what I had to do.

Natanya had freed Celine from her cage and gone for another walk or inside the hut when I returned. Kien was off somewhere too. Wife no. 1 and wife no. 2 were sitting on the stone wall patiently awaiting the return of the herd from their excursion. They were busily plucking the feathers from two large pheasant like birds. Our dinner, I presumed. The arrows with which they had been killed were lying on the ground near the women's feet. I assumed that they had not killed the birds and so I added proficiency with a bow to Kien's array of skills.

I went into the hut to get a goatskin of Kien's high octane, milky brew. The light inside was dim and at first I did not see Celine and Natanya on the far side of the room. Fio, wife no. 3, was with them. Celine was on her knees, her arms still bound behind her and still as naked as the day she was born. Fio was leaning back on her hands, her knees drawn up and her thighs spread. The pretty, brown haired girl had her head between them and had her tongue buried in Fio's wet and dilated canal. Natanya was behind the young girl stroking her quim and issuing her verbal encouragement.

"That's it, Celine, lap up all that delicious juice. Make Fio hot. That's a good girl."

Fio's eyes had been closed, but she must have sensed me standing there since she opened them and gave me a big smile. Natanya looked up too.

"Harry's watching you, Celine. He likes to see you naked and having your cunt serviced. Put on a good show for him, dear."

I heard Celine give a whine of unhappiness at the thought that I was watching her debasement, but she continued to service the moist cleft of the Asian woman. I could tell that Celine was close to the edge of her crisis because I could hear her heavy breath and I could see her hips gyrating and pressing back at the spider woman's hand. Her hands were squirming in her bonds behind her back. Her plump breasts were crushed against her knees. I crouched down so that I could get a better look. My cock yearned to possess the tender slit between her thighs. On the other hand, having her thin lips pursed around my cock would have been fine too. I was jealous of Fio who was beginning to moan and squirm as the young girl drove her to the heights of delight. Her stiffened nipples showed through her thin shift and her mouth hung open.

Celine was nearing her climax. "Don't come yet, Celine, not until Fio does. I wouldn't want to have to punish you," Natanya told her. "I could have Mr. Harry whip you. But maybe you'd like that. Would you like to be whipped by Harry, Celine? Or maybe Kien. I'll bet he's really good with a whip."

The young girl gave a groan of frustration and fear as she fought off the effects of the nimble hand in her crevasse. Her rear cheeks pushed together as she tried to assume control of her mounting lust. She was right on the edge.

Suddenly, Fio gave out a deep, happy moan. She began to thrust her hips at the mouth that was pleasuring her sex and she cried out "Oh! Oh! Oh! Oh!" and then a string of words in her native patois that I did not understand. Celine began to come too, having satisfied her mistress's command. "Ahhhhhhhhhh!" she cried into Fio's throbbing cunt. "Ahhhhhhhhhh! Ahhhhhhhhhhh!" Her body seemed to contract and expand at each convulsion of her pussy's walls.

"Keep sucking! Don't stop!" Natanya shouted at her as she massaged her fevered canal. "Give Fio your tongue!"

Celine buried her head deep within the young Asian woman's thighs. Fio jammed them closed round the naked girl's head as her tremors and shudders overwhelmed her. I could hear Celine's muffled cries from between them. I was afraid that the peasant woman would suffocate the poor girl with her sturdy, heavily muscled legs. But after giving out one more ecstatic shout of pleasure, she fell to her back and released Celine's pretty head.

Natanya pulled her ward erect by tugging on her long, chestnut colored ponytail. Celine's face was smeared with Fio's discharge and her face and upper chest were rosy red from her passion. Her chest rose and fell intently as she tried to recover her breath from her orgasm. Her nipples were hard and pointy.

"Good job, Celine," Natanya told her. "What do you think, Harry? Did she do a good job? Or should I have her whipped?"

The young girl looked at me forlornly and shuddered at the possibility that I would take leather to her flesh. I didn't know what stories Natanya had told her about me, but from the girl's reaction she had been laying it on pretty thick. The young girl was enticing in her post cunnalinguistic pose, fear etched on her face. If I had the pretty, young thing back at Klitzman's island I might just have taken a whip to her flesh, just to see her cry and wail. Not too much mind you, that wasn't my usual style. Just enough to make my cock beg for burial in her flesh. But I wasn't about to do it for the spider woman's delight.

"I don't think that a whipping is necessary, Natanya," I answered her. "Unless it's you we're talking about. I wouldn't mind seeing you dance to a whip. It would teach you some manners."

Natanya laughed. "Go ahead and try it, Harry. You'd be dead before morning."

I believed her. She would cut my throat from ear to ear. Well somebody needed to whip her. I would bide my time.

Natanya caressed Celine's pretty head. "I guess we'll have to ask Kien to whip you, Celine. Maybe after dinner. For the time being though I think I'll put the gag back inside your mouth. You look so becoming with your lips distended and your mouth bulging full." The older woman retrieved the leather ball that had been in the girl's mouth earlier and brought it to her lips. "Open wide, Celine, like a good girl." The ball was just a little bigger than Celine's lips would allow. Natanya pressed on it hard and it began to slip inside. "That's it…. Good…, good…," Natanya intoned as the ball began to disappear. When it finally popped in, to the young girl's obvious dismay, Natanya shouted, "There you go! I knew you could do it!"

The cruel spider woman had been right. Celine did look good with her pale cheeks bulging and her thin lips spread wide. Her lovely brown eyes filled up with tears. Oh, how much I wanted to fuck her. I had had enough and I grabbed the goatskin of devil's brew and went outside. Kien had arrived and he had another brace of the pheasants with him. The horse women were trudging in, having completed their rounds. Kien's middle wife had started a fire in the fireplace and was busily turning a long spit with the two birds cooking on it. Kien tossed the birds he had killed on the ground next to her and he and the older woman turned to the huffing and puffing women on the coffle and shouted "Ya! Ya! Ya! Ya!" waving and clapping their hands. The unfortunate Chinese women obediently turned and headed for the barn, the sturdy old man and his crony wife following them.

Dinner was scrumptious. The pheasants had been covered with some kind of spicy sauce that made my taste buds tingle. There was some kind of millet soup and an assembly of strange, oriental vegetables. I tore into my portion of the birds with my hands and licked my fingers clean. Celine was kneeling next to Natanya, still naked and bound, and her mistress was feeding her bits of meat and vegetables while stroking her pussy from behind with her free hand. The girl was on a slow burn and I could see that she was having difficulty controlling her passions. Wife no. 2 was eyeing me with undisguised lust throughout the meal and as she walked around serving the food, she kept on brushing into me causing me to begin to burn with anticipation of her delights. I had drunk more than a fair share of Kien's brew and I was feeling pretty good.

After dinner was over, I watched as the wives cleaned up. They peeled off what was left of the meat from the bird's bones and the remainder of the vegetables and mashed them up in a large pot. A kind of mush had been simmering on the fire in the middle of the hut and they dumped the almost liquefied meat and vegetables into it and then poured in some goat's milk, mixing it all up. Wife nos. 2 and 3 grabbed the handles of the pot and carried it out of the hut while the senior wife followed them. I guessed that it was dinner for the unfortunate women in the barn. My thoughts turned to the young Chinese woman who was spending her first night there as a beast of burden. Since the women could obviously not chew anything, the mush would be poured or ladled into their mouths. I tried to imagine what it would be like to be reduced to that kind of an existence. I couldn't. Could you?

My mood had changed rapidly from exuberant to maudlin. Kien was sitting across from me and had lit his pipe. The little room was silent except for the muted moans of Celine who was still suffering a delicate, slow torment of her sex by Natanya. I wondered what the future held. The perfidious spider woman's attitude to her charge had seemed to change since we had arrived at Kien's little hamlet. Or was it just that now that she and the young girl were out of the public eye their normal relationship had resumed? I was suspicious of everything that the woman did and said. I was thousands of miles away from home, my life depending on the success of my mysterious journey. And I was surrounded by callous and cruel people that I did not know or trust.

It was Natanya who broke the silence in the dimly lit hut. She spoke to the softly moaning Celine. The girl's head had been tilted back, her eyes closed to slits. She seemed hypnotized by her mistress's caresses. Her delicate, round, pinkish breasts stood out brazenly due to the confinement of her arms behind her. It was odd to have such lasciviously displayed female flesh before me and not be able to touch it at will.

"Celine," Natanya spoke softly, almost in a whisper to the girl. "Don't you think that Kien should be thanked for the delicious dinner he gave us? How can a little slut like you best express her thanks, eh? Do you think that he would like it if you crawled over to him and sucked his cock? I think so. Why don't you go do it now?"

Celine's eyes had popped open at the older woman's suggestion. She looked over at the wizened old man who was sitting before the fire so peacefully. Her unhappy, brown eyes then turned to me as if seeking some kind of intervention. I wasn't about to interfere. Natanya said something to the old man, smiling politely and Kien gave out a grunt of approval. His eyes wandered over the delicate flesh of Natanya's plaything expectantly.

"Kien says he would love to have your lips around his cock, Celine," Natanya said. "Go ahead and give him a nice, thank you blow job."

Celine's face broke out into a grimace and she then dutifully began to crawl over to the old Asian man. He had shifted himself to liberate his cock and he was waiting patiently while the bound girl struggled to go over to him, shifting her weight from knee to knee, traveling slowly over the short distance between them. When she reached him, her head bent to his loins.

Due to their position on the other side of the fire, I could not actually see Celine's tender lips as they brought pleasure to the man's tool. But I could see the man's face soften and his eyes draw closed. I could hear the slurping of the girl's lips and her gasps for breath as she serviced him. Her rear was raised and the beautiful young girl's innocent, twin portals beckoned to me. Her delicate hands, joined behind her back, were clasped tight. Natanya leaned back and smiled with satisfaction at her ward's efforts.

"He's getting your blow job, Harry. You should be nicer to me."

"It's not easy to be nice to someone who tried to have you killed, Natanya," I said, laying my cards on the table.

"You mean the little episode back at the hotel? Is that's what's bothering you? I didn't have anything to do with that."

"If only I could believe you, Natanya," I replied.

"Scout's honor, Harry," the black haired woman retorted. "Cross my heart and hope to die."

"You will die if you try anything like that again," I said.

"Oh, Harry," she responded, "why can't we just be friends? We have a long, hard trip together starting tomorrow and you need me to help you. And you shouldn't be so concerned about Celine, you know. She's just a slut after all. Isn't that what got you in trouble with our fat friend? You have to watch that in your business. You're not allowed to have a heart."

Not allowed to have a heart. The treacherous spider woman had hit the nail on the head. I needed to put all of my feelings away. What did it matter what happened to the unfortunate Celine? How bad was her fate when compared to that of the Chinese girls'? And if Natanya gave her to Kien when we got back from the monastery to shave and brand and add to his coffle of dehumanized women, what was that to me? I looked over at the brown haired head that was bobbing in the old man's lap. His eyes were fluttering and his gnarled hands were locked on top of it urging her to greater endeavor. Every once in a while he would push her face down deep into his loins and I could hear the girl gurgle and whine as his cock pierced her delicate, youthful throat. Her hands would strain at her bonds, desperately trying to pull them apart. The little brown flower between her rear cheeks winked as her body tensed and her lungs yearned for air. Some day, soon perhaps, someone would pierce that tiny aperture with their cock and the girl would cry and whine with pain. Who could tell, maybe it would be me. All I had to do was to be nice to Natanya.

"Okay, Natanya," I said. "You win. I'll play your game. Just don't push me too far. Okay?"

"It's a deal," the perfidious woman answered sweetly.

Kien had reached his moment of truth. He gave out a loud grunt as he came. His hands pressed the girl's head hard down on his cock. Celine whined and cried out muffled protests as she struggled to breathe.

To be continued.